MURDER O[illegible] GE GR[illegible]

A 1920s Cozy Mystery

A Lady Felicity Quick Mystery
Book 1

ROSIE HUNT

This book is a work of fiction. Names, characters, places and incidents are either the product of the author's imagination or are used fictitiously, and any resemblance to actual persons, living or dead, events, or locales is entirely coincidental.

ISBN: 9789083290607

Editing by Effie Wilson

Cover art by DLR Cover Designs

For my mother.

Thank you for leaving those Agatha Christie library hardbacks within my young grasp.

A Note on Language

This book is written in British English. There are two reasons for this: the story is set in England, and I (the author) am British.

Part of my British writing style is the use of s where z is used in American English. For example: organise instead of organize, and paralyse instead of paralyze.

However, you may have noticed that in the blurbs and marketing for this book, it's called a cozy mystery and not a cosy mystery.

This is because the American spelling is standard for the genre. Spelling cozy this way helps people (and algorithms) recognise my book more easily.

But outside of book genres, it's cosy all the way.

Cast of Characters

Quick family

Lady Felicity Quick, journalist

Lord Jasper Quick, Earl of Denbury, editor-in-chief of the Western Daily News and Felicity's brother

Lady Henrietta Quick, Dowager Countess of Denbury, grandmother to Felicity and Jasper

Pip, Felicity's Yorkshire Terrier

Northcote family

Lord Basil Northcote, Viscount of Sittingdon, friend of the Quick family

Lady Penelope Northcote, wife of Lord Northcote and friend of the Quick family

Heather, Lady Penelope's Cocker Spaniel

Inhabitants of Lower Diddleton

Father Gerald Neil, parish priest at All Angels church

Mrs Ruth Fry, village baker

Mr Michael Chesterton, landlord of the Cat and Cream Inn

Mrs Enid Winterpole, widow and member of the Lower Diddleton Plant and Floral Society

Mr Arthur Reeves, retired accountant

Mrs Gladys Broughton, member of the Lower Diddleton Plant and Floral Society

Mr Bernard Fry, village baker

Staff

Miss Janey Whedon, cook's helper at Bradley Court, residence of the Quick family

Mr Liam Finnegan, driver for the Quick family

Mr Jim Coombe, gamekeeper on the Sittingdon Hall estate, residence of the Northcote family

Mr Paul Mayhew, gamekeeper on the Sittingdon Hall estate, residence of the Northcote family

Miss Nora Andrews, maid-of-all-work to Mr Arthur Reeves

Mr Alfred Simmons, butler to the Northcote family

Others

Sergeant Hodgkins, police officer based in the village of Sweetbrooke

Constable Price, police officer based in the village of Sweetbrooke

Mr Alexander Cooper, reporter for the Western Daily News

Mr Alistair McNabb, visitor to Lower Diddleton

Mr Duggan, printer based in the village of Sweetbrooke

Chief Inspector Luscombe, police detective based in the city of Exeter

Extract from the Western Daily News, 1921

Murder and Mystery in Lower Diddleton

Extraordinary events rock a quiet village. Our reporter was there!

LOWER DIDDLETON, June 14 — The green rolling hills and secluded hamlets of East Devon are renowned for their slow pace of life. The village of Lower Diddleton, some twelve miles from the relative hustle-and-bustle of the cathedral city of Exeter, would usually be a prime example of such bucolic bliss.

Yet it was in this unassuming location that a series of extraordinary events took place, events that one more readily associates with cities such as London or Liverpool, or even with the silver screen.

Luckily, the staff of your dedicated and trustworthy regional newspaper — a copy of which you are sensible enough to have in your hands — have investigated the truth of what happened in Lower Diddleton and bring you this extended and very detailed write-up.

Chapter One

BRADLEY COURT, NEAR THE VILLAGE OF LOWER DIDDLETON, EAST DEVON, 11 JUNE 1921

The sky was a bright summer blue, and the sun was peeking over the tall, stately pines at the edge of Bradley Court's formal gardens. On a wrought-iron bench painted a dark, glossy green, Lady Felicity Quick sat enjoying her morning cup of tea with a newspaper spread out before her. Pip, Felicity's faithful and rather domineering Yorkshire Terrier, lay sleeping on the gravel path in front of her, his grey and blond fur shimmering in the sunshine. Beside the bench was a dense camellia bush, its deep pink blooms nodding in the breeze that carried with it the scent of flowers and damp grass.

It had rained the night before — there had apparently been thunder and lightning, although Felicity had slept through it — but the morning sun was now quickly warming the garden. Felicity considered moving into the shade of a nearby yew, only it wouldn't be long before she finished her Earl Grey, and she was keen to get to the end of the article she'd begun before the start of a busy day. *Killer Caught Boarding Train to Scotland* was the lurid headline that had grabbed her attention. Felicity had followed the case from the beginning, when a poor woman had been found strangled in a London hotel. It seemed now that the culprit was none other than her own husband, which was a rather tragic twist to the tale.

"It's not very ladylike, though. Is it, Felicity dear?"

Felicity looked up from her newspaper.

Lady Henrietta Quick, Dowager Countess of Denbury and Felicity's grandmother, was on the other side of the gravel path tending to her prize-winning collection of English shrub roses. Eyes narrowed, syringe in hand, Lady Henrietta stooped closely over her flowers, carefully examining the leaves and stems of the roses, which varied in colour from apricot to deep red, and whose delicious fragrance filled the air.

Despite a full agenda for the day, Felicity had promised to keep her grandmother company in the garden over breakfast. Lady Henrietta preferred to hunt aphids before the sun got too high and risked tingeing her cheeks and the backs of her hands a ghastly pink. Felicity had made it clear to her grandmother she couldn't dally for too long. Her first appointment was in Lower Diddleton, a village connected to Felicity's home both geographically and historically. The boundaries of Bradley Court's estate adjoined those of Lower Diddleton, and the Quick family used to rule over the village, but that was an exceedingly long time ago.

Felicity took a little sip of her tea. "Grandmama, when you say 'ladylike', which definition are you using? That of the Twentieth Century or of the Nineteenth?"

Psst! Lady Henrietta squeezed the plunger on her syringe, sending a jet of soapy water towards a deep pink floribunda and dislodging a colony of aphids from its stem. She stood up straight. Though advanced in years, Felicity's grandmother's posture was still upright and elegant. Her face was wrinkled like a walnut shell, but her lavender-blue eyes were bright. She wore a wide-brimmed straw hat she used only when gardening, and though her dress had a modern dropped waist, its shoe-grazing length was more Queen Victoria than 1921.

"Felicity, dearest," said Lady Henrietta with the deepest of sighs. "I'm not quite as behind the times as you seem to enjoy imagining I am."

"My apologies, Grandmama. You mean to say you have no

problem whatever with my choice to pursue a career? I'd been operating under quite the opposite impression."

Lady Henrietta tutted. "Don't be deliberately obtuse, my dear. It's distinctly unbecoming. You know very well it's not your having a career with which I have a problem. It's the *type* of career you seem intent upon. It's simply not fitting for a lady. Nor any woman, for that matter."

Pip let out a loud snore. If he hadn't been asleep, it might have passed for commentary. Felicity was certainly tired of hearing her grandmother's repeated objections to her new job.

Resigned to finishing the tragic story of the wife killer at some other opportunity, Felicity closed her newspaper. "Are you of the opinion that the work of a journalist isn't suited to a woman, Grandmama? Because as you know, I've been writing society pieces for some time now."

A Red Admiral fluttered past the brim of Lady Henrietta's hat. "Society journalism is different. You speak to people you know about topics appropriate for a lady. I wouldn't even call that a career. It's something more of a..." Lady Henrietta watched the butterfly for a moment as she searched for the right word. "A hobby. And a hobby is so much more ladylike, don't you think?"

Felicity swallowed the last of her tea and placed the cup and saucer on the bench. In doing so, she issued a silent reminder to herself: her grandmother's concerns were an expression of her love and perfectly natural given the role Lady Henrietta had played in Felicity's life.

Felicity's mother, Lady Adelaide Quick, had died when Felicity was just a baby. Lady Henrietta had betrayed her own stiff upper lip to fill the void left in Felicity's life. Although Felicity had almost no memories of her mother, Lady Henrietta often told her she'd inherited her mother's auburn curls, hazel eyes, and zest for life, which was enormously comforting.

After Felicity's father sadly passed away not long after the Great War, Lady Henrietta redoubled her efforts to offer Felicity support and advice wherever needed, and Felicity adored and admired her grandmother all the more for it. Bridging the gap between Lady Henrietta's Victorian upbringing and Felicity's development as a young woman in the modern era was no mean feat. But at twenty-one years old, Felicity was now a woman in her own right. It hurt that her chosen career could be dismissed as a hobby, no matter how well-meaning her grandmother was trying to be.

Felicity stood up, stroked down the skirt of her pale green cotton day dress, and adjusted her straw cloche. "Perhaps you could look at it another way, Grandmama. Tradition is important to any family, isn't it? I'm doing my bit in continuing the long line of Quick journalists. Doesn't that make you proud?"

Lady Henrietta's forehead creased under the wide brim of her hat. "But what of the parish newsletter? Don't you find it a terrible shame to give that up? It's been a most rewarding pastime. You've dedicated a tremendous amount of effort to it, and the vicar will be terribly disappointed."

Her grandmother had a point. However, it was one that Felicity had already considered.

During the Great War, and in the absence of the many men called up to fight, Felicity had volunteered for Lower Diddleton's parish newsletter, much to the delight of Father Gerald Neil, who'd been struggling to continue the publication with so few contributors. After the war, Felicity continued her work for the newsletter, even being elevated to the position of editor. In fifteen years, Felicity had been the only person brave enough to confront Mr Broughton, a long-term contributor to the newsletter and an amateur archaeology enthusiast. She reduced his submissions by several thousand words apiece. The result was a rather noticeable boost in circulation.

"Leaving the newsletter is rather a shame," admitted Felicity. "But it was only meant to be temporary. Father Neil can't be disappointed in me for that, and nor do I have any regrets. It's been valuable experience and a stepping stone to something more exciting."

Lady Henrietta tutted again. "Excitement, indeed. If only your parents were here. One can only imagine what they'd have to say about all this."

Pip let out another snore, this one more befitting of a gorilla than a small terrier.

Felicity smiled mischievously. "I was too young to know my mother well, but I gather she was the progressive sort. She'd have surely favoured a woman's right to choose her own career. Is that not so?"

Lady Henrietta huffed and waved her syringe, spraying a little arc of soapy water into the air. "Your father, then. Kingsley simply wouldn't have allowed it. He didn't, in fact."

This was true. Felicity's father and Lady Henrietta's eldest son, the late Lord Kingsley Quick, had not only been the Earl of Denbury, he'd also been the owner and editor-in-chief of the Quick family's newspaper until his death two years ago. Since 1858, the Western Daily News had been reporting on matters from Bristol to Penzance, and ever since she was a little girl, Felicity yearned to be part of it. She loved to write, was fascinated by newspapers, and thoroughly enjoyed interviewing people, but her father had been adamant. Except for secretarial roles — which wasn't any kind of work for the upper classes — the world of newspapers was no place for women.

Not that Lord Kingsley thought Felicity incapable. He loved Felicity very much and brought her up to be a confident and intelligent young woman, capable of forming her own opinions and expressing them eloquently. He simply didn't like the idea of any woman, let alone his own daughter, becoming mixed up in news reporting. As Lord Kingsley saw it, to deliver the truth, journalists had to come into contact with the murkier side of life, which women ought to be shielded from. Her father's duty was therefore to protect Felicity from ever becoming a journalist.

Things changed when Felicity's brother, Lord Jasper Quick, the current Earl of Denbury, took control of the Western Daily News upon their father's death. Jasper was just a few years older than Felicity and far less old-fashioned than their father. He was also too busy with his new role at the newspaper, which involved a great deal of travel across the region and much placating of the publication's advertisers, to put up a strong defence in response to his younger sister's pleading.

After a respectable period of mourning for their father had passed, Jasper assigned Felicity the role of society reporter at the Western Daily News. Then, just a couple of weeks ago, he'd given into further pestering and conceded his younger sister a promotion. Felicity was now a news reporter and would be given her first assignment that very day. She could barely wait.

The grandfather clock in Bradley Court's hall marked eight o'clock, its gentle chimes floating through open windows and into the garden. Felicity needed to leave soon if she was to be on time for the day's first meeting.

"You're right about father, Grandmama," she said in an appeasing tone. "And you so often are right about things, but I promise there's absolutely no need to worry about me. Jasper keeps a close eye, and the world is different to how it was in father's time. Or in your time, for that matter."

Felicity's grandmother looked at her with suspicion. "Your brother cares for you very much, but he's also a very busy man. He can't keep watch over you around the clock."

And thank goodness for that, added Felicity silently as she carefully made her way through the rose bushes towards her grandmother.

Lady Henrietta cleared her throat a little before continuing. "And I know I promised not to mention it again, but just look at what happened at Wolborne House."

"Wolborne House was quite exceptional," said Felicity. "That's absolutely not what I mean by excitement. I've no desire to experience anything like that again." Felicity lifted the brim of Lady Henrietta's hat and kissed her on both cheeks. "Really, Grandmama, I must go. I can't be late to meet the vicar."

Lady Henrietta narrowed her lavender-blue eyes at Felicity. "Be careful, my dear."

Felicity suppressed an incredulous lift of her brow, for what dramatic or dangerous event had ever happened in Lower Diddleton? "I will be," said Felicity brightly with a wave, aware that humouring her grandmother was the best approach if she was ever to make it into the village on time. "I always am."

Mussing the fur on his little head, Felicity collected a slightly discombobulated Pip, who had been sleeping rather deeply, and with the yawning Yorkie at her heels, she crossed the wide, neatly clipped lawn to the wooden stile in the dry-stone wall where Bradley Court's gardens connected with the lane to the village.

Chapter Two

With Pip now fully awake and trotting ahead of her, Felicity walked briskly towards Lower Diddleton. The lane winding into the village was flanked with swathes of bright red poppies and dense green hedgerow from which a sweet cacophony of birdsong emanated. Beyond the hedgerows lay the undulating East Devon countryside, a patchwork of bright green fields stretching towards the horizon. The rain overnight had given the land a rich, earthy smell, but thankfully, there weren't too many puddles. Felicity had on a pair of rather new dark green t-strap shoes, the green of which matched the trimmings on her dress and the ribbon around her hat.

A tuneful whistle drifted along the lane. At a break in a hedgerow, beyond a large wooden gate, a group of agricultural workers were collecting cherries from a sprawling orchard. From the tops of ladders, the men lifted their caps, and Felicity smiled at them. The morning was so pleasant, she'd almost forgotten that she would shortly have a conversation with Father Neil that would lead to disappointment on his part. Felicity hated letting people down, but she couldn't be both a news journalist for her brother's paper and the editor of the parish newsletter. There simply wasn't the time.

A familiar figure appeared in the lane. It was Janey, one of the kitchen maids at Bradley Court. Short with dark hair and rosy cheeks, Janey carried a wicker basket on her arm and was walking so fast she was in danger of breaking into a run. Drawing closer to Felicity, the kitchen maid stopped abruptly and bobbed a speedy curtsey. Pip put his little black nose in the air and sniffed, in case anything in the basket might interest a small dog with a penchant for sausages.

"Good morning, my lady," Janey said somewhat breathlessly. She had a melodious accent from Northeast England that Felicity thought quite lovely. "Good morning, Master Pip."

"Good morning, Janey. Don't let me hold you up. It seems Cook's sent you on an urgent errand."

"Yes, my lady. Cook was hoping to serve raspberry tarts at afternoon tea today, only the magpies got to our crop in the kitchen garden, so she sent me down to the village to see if I could find any in the shops. I found a few, but I had to take some strawberries just in case it weren't enough. I hope Cook's not disappointed."

"Cook will understand, Janey," said Felicity reassuringly. "She's a reasonable woman, and strawberries do combine rather well with raspberries. Now, don't let me hold you up any longer."

"Yes, my lady. Thank you, my lady." Janey curtseyed again. "I suppose you're in a hurry yourself. For the meeting."

Felicity frowned a little. "What meeting might that be?"

"There's a group gathered on the village green. I thought that might be where you're heading, my lady."

Felicity didn't need to see the gathering to know exactly what it was about. Every year, Lower Diddleton held a summer fete, and every year, there were squabbles among the organising committee members about how it should be arranged. Felicity could already picture which of the village's strongly opinionated residents had got up early to gather on the green and disagree with one another. Lady Henrietta occasionally dragged Felicity along to related meetings, such as those held by Lower Diddleton's Plant and Floral Society, but it was never by choice that Felicity attended such events. She was by nature more of an observer than a participator.

"Oh, no," said Felicity. "That meeting has nothing to do with me, I assure you."

Thanking Janey for the warning, Felicity continued towards the village. Even if she wanted to take part in the disagreements about the summer fete, there simply wasn't the time for it. First, Felicity had her early appointment with the vicar. Then, at nine o'clock, she was scheduled to meet her brother Jasper for her first assignment as a news journalist. Writing about who would enter their marrows for the largest vegetable prize or where the fete's coconut shy would be situated was no longer Felicity's concern. As a news reporter, Felicity could from now on be sent anywhere in the Westcountry to investigate and write stories of regional importance.

After a bend in the lane at which Pip insisted on being picked up and tucked under Felicity's arm, the village of Lower Diddleton came into view, as familiar as the face of an old friend. There was All Angels church with its sharp grey spire, a small row of pastel-coloured shops, and the Cat and Cream Inn, which was a rather unusual name, even by Devonian standards. Then there were the cottages occupied by the village's residents, most of which were whitewashed with thatched roofs and gardens bursting with summer flowers. But the real heart of Lower Diddleton was its village green. Dotted with trees, including some majestic and very ancient oaks, the green had a cricket pitch, several benches, and a recently arrived white telephone box at its far end.

Just as Janey had said, a cluster of people were standing near the green's duck pond, but it was immediately apparent it wasn't a summer fete committee gathering. Father Neil stood out among the group, his long, willowy frame and wisps of grey hair unmistakable. With him were Mrs Ruth Fry, the baker's wife, Mr Michael Chesterton, the landlord of the Cat and Cream, and Mrs Enid Winterpole, who was the only person present from the summer fete committee.

Perhaps Mrs Winterpole was touting for new committee members? It seemed rather early in the day for it. Whatever the reason for their meeting, Felicity hoped the villagers wouldn't find it rude that she would call the vicar away, as she'd already scheduled their discussion via telephone the day before, and she was on rather a tight schedule.

"Good morning," Felicity said cheerily, approaching the group.

Upon seeing her, Father Neil gestured with his hands for her not to come any further. "Stop, please, Lady Felicity. You mustn't come here. Really, you mustn't."

Felicity didn't alter her course. Time was of the essence. "My apologies, father, but we have a meeting, remember?"

"Really, my lady." Father Neil waved his hands more frantically. "I must insist that you stay away."

"What is it?" asked Felicity with a smile. "A new batch of flag irises for the duck pond? The introduction of a black swan or two?"

She craned her neck as Pip's nose twitched. The villagers liked to arrange surprises. One year, they dug a bed of begonias spelling the village's name. It was a hit with day-trippers. There had even been a surge in popularity when the plants began dying back and the display for a time read 'Low Diddle'.

"It's not possible to keep a secret in Lower Diddleton for very long," continued Felicity. "You must know that."

"I can only agree with the vicar, Lady Felicity." Mr Chesterton, landlord of the Cat and Cream, stepped forward, holding a hand out firmly to ward Felicity off. He was as lean as the vicar, but nowhere near as tall. He had a thin, dark moustache and not much hair left on his head. "It's best you don't come any closer," he said in his nasally voice.

There was a light rumble in Pip's chest as the little dog growled at Mr Chesterton.

"Come now," said Felicity, lightly. "Excluding me from whatever you're all up to is hardly in keeping with the village spirit, is it? And besides, I'm afraid I've come to collect Father Neil. He and I are meeting this morning."

But as she continued towards the group, and the pale-cheeked, wide-eyed faces of Mrs Fry and Mrs Winterpole turned towards her,

Felicity finally realised why Father Neil and Mr Chesterton had been doing their best to warn her away. Only it was too late.

She froze.

On the ground, face-down in the muddy grass at the edge of the duck pond, lay a portly man of about forty years of age. He had black, brilliantined hair, the metal frame of his glasses was twisted, and his jacket was soaked, as if he'd been lying there all night in the rain. Hints of blue were present in the ghostly whiteness of his skin.

Felicity tightened her hold on Pip as a wave of alarm spread through her.

"Oh, dear," she said. "He's dead, isn't he?"

Chapter Three

Rather regrettably, it wasn't the first dead body Felicity had seen in her twenty-one years, but she never expected to come upon one in Lower Diddleton. Definitely not that morning. And certainly not at the edge of the now-empty duck pond, the ducks having fled.

Felicity swallowed. "It's Mr Reeves, is it not?"

The vicar nodded. "Sadly, my lady, it is. Mr Arthur Reeves. Not the way one would expect the life of a retired accountant to end. Tragic. Utterly tragic."

Felicity didn't know Mr Reeves well. She wondered if anyone in Lower Diddleton did. He wasn't particularly outgoing, and as inhabitants of the village went, he was rather new, having acquired the old blacksmith's cottage only a couple of years back. It had one of the largest gardens in the village, stretching right up to the Northcote estate.

"He, ah..." Felicity struggled to know what to say. "Mr Reeves was quite keen on his garden, wasn't he?" As the words came out, she realised she wasn't saying anything useful, but was there anything useful one could say?

Mrs Winterpole spoke gently in response. "That's right, dear." She was a small, frail-looking woman of around seventy, with puffy white hair and a careful way of speaking. She wore a lilac dress and a wide-brimmed hat in a matching shade, and she had in her hand a small bunch of purple and yellow flowers. "Mr Reeves filled his garden with a selection of quite unusual plants. Exotics, I suppose one would call them. He brought seedlings to Plant and Floral Society meetings on a couple of occasions, but none of us knew what to do with them." She shook her head sadly. "I'm afraid Mr Reeves gave up on us after that."

Felicity stroked Pip. The familiar smoothness of his fur was reassuring. "And how did Mr Reeves..." She nodded towards the body. "Meet his, um, end?"

"Gunshot, if you ask me," said Mr Chesterton, pointing dispassionately at the dead man's back. "There's a hole in his jacket. His clothes are wet from the rain we had last night, but I'd say that dark patch there is blood."

Felicity lifted her eyebrows, a little taken aback by this gruesome detail. "Did anyone see what happened?"

The landlord shook his head. "None of us saw anything. And I doubt anyone heard anything either, not with that almighty storm last night."

"Was it, do you think..." Felicity couldn't keep the idea to herself. "Murder?"

Mrs Fry let out a sob and turned her head away. A stout woman of about forty in a white apron, she still had flour in her hair, which was swept back into a tight bun.

Mr Chesterton shrugged. He seemed rather relaxed about the whole affair. "It looks like a nasty sort of business, but the police are on their way over from Sweetbrooke. I'm sure they'll sort it all out." He frowned, still peering at the body. "Although I doubt they'll have the matter cleared up in time for the summer fete. It's going to be terrible for takings at the inn."

Mrs Fry wept, her thick shoulders heaving. Father Neil fetched a handkerchief from his pocket and offered it to her. Felicity's discussion with the vicar about her position on the parish newsletter would have to wait as Mr Reeves' death would no doubt keep Father Neil very busy indeed.

"Who discovered the body?" asked Felicity.

Mrs Winterpole stepped forward. "That would be me, dear."

Although not as hard-hearted as the pub landlord, Mrs Winterpole's composure in the presence of her dead neighbour was steely next to that of Mrs Fry. For Felicity, this was unsurprising. She'd witnessed Mrs Winterpole's firebrand performances at local committee meetings and knew her genteel frailty to be rather misleading.

"And I'm afraid it's quite my fault that poor Mrs Fry is here at all," continued Mrs Winterpole. "I was on my way to the churchyard with fresh flowers for my beloved Kenneth when I saw something by the pond. I took a quick look, but I was worried my eyes might have been playing tricks on me. When one gets to my age, one can't be too sure. So I went to fetch someone who I hoped would reassure me I was simply seeing things. Mrs Fry from the bakery was kind enough to assist. I'd hoped it might be a scarecrow blown out of a farmer's field during the storm. Only it wasn't that at all. It was poor Mr Reeves."

Pip struggled in Felicity's arms. He wanted to be put on the ground, but a little dog sniffing around the dead body would be rather disrespectful, so she tightened her grip on the Yorkie, signalling to him he would have to wait.

Mr Chesterton chimed in, his hands on his hips. "I was putting the signs out at the front of the inn when I saw Mrs Fry accompany Mrs Winterpole to the pond, and I thought nothing of it. But when Mrs Fry let out a cry — well, it was more of a wail, really — I came straight over. As soon as I realised what had happened, I went back to the inn and telephoned for the police. I didn't bother summoning the doctor. Didn't see any point. The man was clearly dead. Then I went to fetch the vicar."

Felicity looked at Father Neil, waiting for him to add his part to the story. The vicar nodded somewhat stiffly, glancing uneasily at the dead body on the ground before them. "It was too late for me or for anyone, really, to be of any use to poor Mr Reeves," he said, his voice shaking a little. "But I can at least be of assistance to Mrs Fry here and to anyone else seeking reassurance at this dark moment for Lower Diddleton." He turned to the sobbing woman and put a comforting hand on her shoulder. "Come, Mrs Fry. Allow me to escort you back to the bakery. Is there someone else who can run the counter for you this morning? Your husband, perhaps? I recommend you take a lie down. You've had quite a shock."

Mrs Fry's weeping only intensified.

Mrs Winterpole put a hand to her mouth as the vicar started towards the bakery with Mrs Fry. "I feel quite responsible," she said. "I really do. If it hadn't been for me, the poor woman wouldn't have been involved. You can't really see the duck pond from the bakery window. Poor Mrs Fry seems to have taken it rather badly. I'd imagined her to be made of stronger stuff. Had I known she'd go to pieces, I'd never have troubled her."

Again Pip struggled to free himself from Felicity's arms. She gave him a gentle squeeze, and he settled. "Please, Mrs Winterpole," she said. "You mustn't blame yourself. The only person to carry any guilt in this matter is whoever did this horrifying deed."

Mrs Winterpole looked up at Felicity. "That's what it is, then? Murder?"

Mr Chesterton leaned over the body, his hands still on his hips. For Felicity's liking, he was standing rather close to what should have been left untouched as a crime scene for investigation, though she didn't feel it her place to say.

"I'd say so," said the inn's landlord. "Whoever did it must have had a good reason. Quite a risky move, murder in the middle of the village like that."

Felicity arced an eyebrow. "Might you know of a reason someone wanted Mr Reeves done away with, Mr Chesterton?"

"No," he blurted, fixing Felicity with a wide-eyed stare. "No, I certainly didn't."

Mrs Winterpole nodded as though in agreement. "I don't think any of us knew Mr Reeves particularly well. He came to the occasional committee meeting, of course, but even then, he wasn't terribly forthcoming. A quiet man, really."

"It's the quiet ones you've got to watch out for," muttered the inn landlord, as he stepped around the body, examining it from all angles.

Felicity was about to ask for clarification on Mr Chesterton's mumbled comment when the sound of a fast-moving motor car stole everyone's attention. The dark blue Model T drew up on the grass on the other side of the pond, and two uniformed police officers got out, one ginger-haired and tall, the other older and somewhat rotund, with a thick moustache. Felicity recognised them as Constable Price and Sergeant Hodgkins from the police station at Sweetbrooke, a village slightly larger than Lower Diddleton on the road towards Exeter. Mrs Winterpole glared scathingly at the deep, muddy tyre tracks now etched into the green's neatly kept grass.

The landlord's back straightened as the two police officers approached. "Morning, lads," he said with inappropriate familiarity and jolliness.

Pip gave a last struggle for freedom, emitting a small yap as he twisted out of Felicity's grip, leaving her no choice but to lower him to the ground. She imagined that the little dog may have personal business to attend to, but no. He immediately scampered off towards the body and began sniffing at the dead man's clothes.

"Pip!" Felicity hissed as she started off after the wayward terrier. She did her best not to add too many extra footprints to the scene of the crime, but were Pip to empty the dead man's pockets looking for treats, Felicity would have died of embarrassment. "Pip! Come here this instant!"

The little dog was sniffing his way up the dead man's trouser leg when Felicity lunged for him. Pip easily evaded his mistress and moved towards Mr Reeves' shoulder, sniffing as he went, seemingly intent on collecting every trace of scent from the corpse.

"Pip! Your behaviour is unacceptable!"

The chase brought Felicity closer to the dead man, and she saw details she hadn't noticed before. There was indeed a small hole in the back of his jacket, but whether it was the entry or exit point for a bullet, Felicity couldn't tell. She also saw that Mr Reeves had been dressed rather casually at the time of his demise. His shoes were a battered pair of brogues, and he had on no tie. She tried to avoid looking at his face, as the dead man's rather strained expression and open eyes gave Felicity quite a queer feeling.

With Pip now thoroughly engaged in sniffing the man's armpit, Felicity saw her chance and stepped forward to grab him, avoiding Mr Reeves' arm, which was outstretched at an unusual angle. "Got you!" said Felicity, as she scooped Pip up and tucked him under her arm. Before retreating with the captured Yorkie, she allowed her gaze to follow the dead man's outstretched limb to his hand. It was balled into a fist except for an extended index finger, the tip of which was pressed into the soft, red mud at the edge of the duck pond.

Felicity blinked.

Under the dead man's finger, drawn in the mud, was a single letter.

The letter N.

Chapter Four

Their silver badges and buttons flashing in the morning sun, the two police officers strode towards the dead body. Mr Chesterton buzzed around them like a fly.

"An inquest, you say? To be held at my inn?"

"That would be the usual run of things, Mr Chesterton," replied Sergeant Hodgkins without looking at the innkeeper, his round face grave.

Felicity stepped back from the body, Pip tightly clamped under her arm. Had she been carrying her camera, she could have captured the letter in the mud and ensured it wouldn't be lost, but her camera had been damaged by rain just recently and had been sent back to the shop for repairs. Besides, the police were here now. They would take care of everything.

"Officers," said Felicity, pointing to the N by the corpse's hand as the policemen approached the body. "I believe there's something quite important here."

"Everybody stand back," said Sergeant Hodgkins loudly, as though addressing a large crowd. "We need to preserve the scene. Please vacate the area."

The police officers split up, one on either side of the dead body.

Constable Price barged past Felicity, his freckled nose wrinkled with a whiff of distaste as he surveyed the corpse.

"Really, officers," Felicity protested. "I think there's something you need to see, and you ought to be careful, otherwise—"

With a squelch, Constable Price's boot landed in the mud at the edge of the pond. A single duck that had been hiding in the reeds flew quacking into the air.

Felicity's voice trailed off. "—you might tread on it."

The constable's boot had come down close to Mr Reeves' hand, leaving a deep footprint in the mud. The letter N was no more.

"We've a job to do here," continued Sergeant Hodgkins, who was now threshing the reeds with his truncheon, presumably to flush out any further hidden ducks. "So we'd appreciate it if you all returned to your respective homes."

"But you just—" began Felicity, but she was cut off.

"We know where to find you, and we'll be along presently to gather your witness statements," said the sergeant, who was now squinting into the pond.

Mrs Winterpole frowned. "I witnessed nothing at all. I merely found Mr Reeves in his current state."

The sergeant straightened himself and came to stand over the body, his hands on his hips. "This is a crime scene, and Constable Price and I have a duty to protect it until the detective branch arrives from Exeter. Now—" he lifted his truncheon towards the village high street "—if you'd be so kind as to leave the area."

The innkeeper rubbed his hands together. "And the inquest takes place in a couple of days, you say?"

"That's not the most important thing right now," said Sergeant Hodgkins with the air of an exasperated schoolmaster. "If you'd please all return to your homes and allow us to continue our work."

"Of course, gents. Of course," said Mr Chesterton, retreating obsequiously towards his inn on the far side of the green. "You know where to find me. The Cat and Cream is open all day from Monday to Saturday, and every Sunday afternoon."

Pausing beside Felicity, Mrs Winterpole sighed. "Terrible business. I'm glad my Kenneth isn't around to see it. A murder in Lower Diddleton. I'd never have imagined it possible."

With a shake of her head, Mrs Winterpole began walking towards the church, leaving a rather speechless Felicity, Pip still under her arm, to watch the two police officers continuing to 'secure' the crime scene.

She considered another attempt at raising the now-erased letter in the mud, but another motor pulled onto the formerly immaculate grass of the village green, presumably with reinforcements from the police headquarters at Exeter, and Sergeant Hodgkins went marching towards it, Constable Price hastily following in his superior's wake.

Felicity bit gently on her lip as she considered her options. Her resignation from the parish newsletter would have to wait, but that was the least of her concerns. There'd been a murder in Lower Diddleton, and just like Mrs Winterpole, Felicity would never have imagined it possible, yet the victim of the dreadful crime still lay on the grass before her.

Jasper would no doubt want the story covered in the Western Daily News. Felicity was surely well-positioned to write such an article, having rather thorough knowledge of Lower Diddleton and its residents as well as good access to anyone she wished to speak to locally.

The clock on the church tower told Felicity it was five-and-twenty to nine. There was still time before her nine o'clock appointment with Jasper.

With Pip still tucked under her arm, Felicity strode away from the village green. She was a news reporter now, and it was time to conduct her first interview.

Mrs Winterpole was standing by the old wooden lychgate at the entrance to the churchyard when Felicity caught up with her. She was talking to Mrs Broughton, a woman of similar age to Mrs Winterpole who lived with her amateur-archaeologist husband in a cottage on the road towards Sweetbrooke. With their pastel-toned hats nodding in the sunshine, from a distance, the two women looked like spring flowers dancing in the breeze. But Mrs Broughton's expression was pained, her eyes darting towards the village green, where more cars were now arriving. News about Mr Reeves' demise was spreading.

Felicity placed Pip on the ground. He'd been well-behaved since she scooped him up from the murder scene, but if she insisted on holding onto him without good reason, his amiable mood wouldn't last. As Pip sniffed the bright yellow dandelions protruding from the bottom of the churchyard's grey stone wall, Felicity approached Mrs Winterpole and Mrs Broughton.

"Oh, how absolutely awful," said Mrs Broughton, bringing a hand to her cheek, an empty wicker shopping basket in the crook of her arm. "And the police have no idea who shot the poor man?"

"At this stage, I doubt they have more of a clue than we do," said Mrs Winterpole, the rather attractive posy of purple and yellow flowers still in her hand. She looked towards Felicity. "Wouldn't you say so, Lady Felicity?"

Felicity remembered the squelch of the younger policeman's boot in the mud and considered saying that the police had perhaps even less of a clue, but she kept the thought to herself. "Indeed, Mrs Winterpole," she said. "That's the impression I came away with as well."

Mrs Broughton's gaze wandered again to the village green. There were in total three motors now parked on the grass and around a dozen men, some in police uniform, some in plain clothes, busying themselves at the scene of Mr Reeves' fateful collapse. A stiff, white sheet had been draped over the dead man's body.

"Oh, how horrible," said Mrs Broughton. "You might expect such a thing in Bristol or Plymouth, or even in Exeter. But here, in Little Diddleton?" She shook her head. "It's unthinkable."

"Yet it happened," said Mrs Winterpole with a sad sigh.

"You were the first to come upon the body, were you not, Mrs

Winterpole?" Felicity asked. As she spoke, she drew a small reporter's notebook and silver mechanical pencil from the pocket of her dress. Through her work on the parish newsletter, the villagers were accustomed to seeing Felicity with her pencil in her hand, and she was never without the means to take notes.

"I suppose so," Mrs Winterpole said. "Although I've no way of knowing that for certain. Whoever did for the poor man would have been on the scene before me, of course. Will you be writing this up for the parish newsletter, Lady Felicity?"

"I'm considering writing an article on the matter, yes," Felicity said somewhat evasively, not wanting to announce her resignation from the newsletter and new position on the Western Daily News before having informed the vicar.

"That's a splendid idea," said Mrs Winterpole. "It'll be just what the village needs after such a terrible shock. You write so wonderfully well, Lady Felicity. I'm sure you'll be able to help us make sense of this tragedy."

Felicity nodded demurely. Her article would hopefully benefit the parish, regardless of which publication it appeared in. "Did you notice anything..." She considered the right word to use. "Anything unusual about the scene?"

"Unusual, dear?" Mrs Winterpole wrinkled her nose. "You mean aside from there being a dead man on our quiet village's usually peaceful green?"

Felicity's cheeks flushed a little as she wrote down Mrs Winterpole's comments in a brisk Pitman shorthand. Her question had perhaps not been worded carefully enough, but she didn't want to tell Mrs Winterpole about the letter N in the mud. She was merely curious to know if Mrs Winterpole had seen it too, and if there were any other clues she had noticed that Felicity had missed, clues that had perhaps been destroyed by one of the other villagers that had arrived on the scene. Mr Chesterton of the Cat and Cream hadn't been particularly careful around the body.

Felicity cleared her throat a little. "I meant, Mrs Winterpole, did you see anything unusual about the body? Perhaps how it was lying, or anything on the ground next to it."

Mrs Winterpole thought for a moment. "No, Lady Felicity. I can't say that I did. But then I rather suspect I wouldn't have noticed. As I told you, at first, my eyes aren't as good as they once were. Why, I wouldn't have even seen that poor Mr Reeves had been shot were it not for Mr Chesterton coming over and telling us so."

Mrs Broughton shook her head. "Poor Mr Reeves. Such a polite, quiet man. I used to see him out walking quite regularly. There's a view of Venny Woods from our back garden, and Mr Broughton and I would often see Mr Reeves out there for his evening walk, rain or shine, and always alone. Such a solitary soul. He did no one any harm."

Mrs Winterpole huffed. "Now, Gladys. I wouldn't go so far as to say that about Mr Reeves."

Felicity lifted her pencil from her notepad. "Did Mr Reeves hurt someone, Mrs Winterpole?"

"I wouldn't quite say that, either," said Mrs Winterpole. "All I know is that not everyone was especially keen on Mr Reeves' choice of garden plants."

Mrs Broughton frowned deeply. "Really, Enid. I know passions sometimes run high at the Lower Diddleton Plant and Floral Society, but surely no one's ever considered murder over planting schemes?"

"The incident to which I'm referring wasn't a question of taste, Gladys," said Mrs Winterpole with an impatient tut. "I understand that one of Mr Reeves' more exotic specimens made a horse kept in a neighbouring field rather ill."

Felicity raised an eyebrow and looked across the village green at Mr Reeves' cottage. The front garden with its bright yellow gate was just visible beyond a stand of trees at the green's edge. With large palmate leaves and spiky fronds in all shades of green, Mr Reeves' choice of planting for his front garden certainly wasn't typical of an English country cottage.

"In the neighbouring field..." Mrs Broughton repeated thoughtfully. "Oh. You mean on Lord Northcote's land?"

The Northcote estate was on the opposite side of Lower Diddleton to the Quick estate. Over the centuries, the two families had been bitter enemies, but allegiances developed during the English Civil War had made them allies for generations. The current Lord Northcote had been a close friend of Felicity's father. Felicity knew him affectionately as Uncle Basil, and there were two things Uncle Basil cared deeply about: hunting and his horses.

"Exactly, Gladys," said Mrs Winterpole. "I believe the mare in question became so sick Lord Northcote thought he would lose her. The animal survived, but he ceased using the field bordering Mr Reeves' garden altogether after that. I understand Lord Northcote was quite upset about the whole affair."

Felicity couldn't ignore two rather unfortunate facts: Northcote began with N, and Lord Northcote certainly owned a gun. He owned several, in fact, and held shooting parties whenever the seasons allowed for it, but it was unthinkable that Uncle Basil would commit such a terrible crime and especially not over a plant. Even if he were driven to murder, would Lord Northcote leave his victim in the middle of Lower Diddleton, for everyone to see? Surely he'd be more discreet.

"Are you saying Mr Reeves was murdered for having the wrong plants in his garden?" said Mrs Broughton with a slight undertone of alarm, as though worried she may have an offending plant or two in her own borders.

"No, Gladys," said Mrs Winterpole a little condescendingly. "I'm not suggesting for one moment that Lord Northcote is a murderer. I'm simply pointing out that Mr Reeves was perhaps not as harmless as he might have seemed. I'm aware it can be unbecoming to speak ill of the dead, but at my age, death is difficult to hold in high regard."

Felicity continued to write in her notebook as she spoke. "Mr Reeves didn't poison Lord Northcote's horses on purpose, though, did he?"

"I doubt that very much," replied Mrs Winterpole. "But one has a responsibility to one's neighbours, does one not?"

"Did Mr Reeves have any enemies besides Lord Northcote?" asked Felicity.

"I really wouldn't know," said Mrs Winterpole. "And I'd prefer to avoid referring to Lord Northcote as the dead man's enemy. We wouldn't want the police to get the wrong idea, would we?"

Felicity smiled somewhat apologetically and swallowed. Mrs Winterpole had made rather a good point.

"You could try talking to Mr Reeves' maid," suggested Mrs Broughton. "She might know more, although she's a timid little thing. Rather young and naïve, even for a maid. I wonder what the police will get out of her."

Felicity looked again toward Mr Reeves' cottage. Two men in overcoats and trilby hats, presumably freshly arrived detectives, were entering the garden gate.

"It'll be a terrible shock for the young girl," said Mrs Winterpole. "For one's employer to be murdered is not at all how a domestic prefers to finish in a position. I'm certain of that."

"It's a terrible shock for everyone in Lower Diddleton," said Mrs Broughton. "Why, I'm not even sure I can continue with my morning errands. It's rather a queer feeling, knowing that one of our neighbours has been killed and that his body is still lying there, on our village green."

Mrs Winterpole shook her head sadly. "The village may never be the same after this. It wouldn't surprise me if our summer fete had to be cancelled altogether."

Felicity listened politely as the two women lamented the efforts that would go to waste should the fete be cancelled. Mrs Broughton's husband had spent many weeks growing what he hoped would be prize-winning onions, and Mrs Winterpole had cultivated some very special roses for the occasion, but as the church bells struck a quarter to nine, it was time for Felicity to return to Bradley Court for the meeting with her brother.

She took leave of Mrs Winterpole and Mrs Broughton, tucking her notepad back into her pocket and calling Pip to heel, which was a command he pretended to only vaguely understand but to which he generally responded, preferring not to be left behind. Passing the still-growing police presence on the village green, an odd little frisson passed through Felicity. Jasper doubtlessly already had a reporting assignment in mind for her, but he would not yet have heard about Mr Reeves' murder. As she hurried down the lane towards Bradley Court, Felicity's excitement grew as she imagined what a scoop her first assignment as a news reporter would be.

Chapter Five

Felicity and Pip went their separate ways in the cool, voluminous entrance hall of Bradley Court. Felicity's family home had been a monastery for hundreds of years before being converted into a Tudor manor house. It wasn't as imposing from the outside as some other stately homes, but it was a sprawling residence, with the various chapels and dormitories of the monastery still part of the layout, albeit repurposed and redecorated many times across the centuries.

Whenever Pip was awake, he made it his business to be with Felicity as much as possible. But when it came to sleeping, and he napped rather frequently, his favourite place on a warm day was in the shade of a large, white-flowered viburnum at the back of the house. There, Pip would snooze while keeping a half-open eye on the kitchen door. That way, he rarely missed a visit from the village butcher's boy, who always carried a few off-cuts for any dogs he met on his delivery rounds.

As Pip's paws tapped across the black-and-white tiles of Bradley Court's entrance hall, Felicity made straight for the corridor that connected the Tudor manor house to what had once been the monastery's cloister. Her footsteps beating a steady rhythm on the thinly carpeted floorboards, and with the faces of her ancestors peering down from portraits that adorned the walls, Felicity mentally completed the list of reasons she would present to Jasper for why she should cover the story of Mr Reeves' murder: Felicity was an experienced journalist who was local to the area, she'd arrived early at the scene of the crime, and she'd already interviewed Mrs Winterpole, a key witness and the first to discover the body. Confident that her brother would agree with her reasoning, Felicity imagined she'd shortly be hurrying back to the village to conduct more interviews.

Upon arriving precisely on time at the dark oak door of Jasper's study, it came as a surprise to hear her brother already occupied with someone else. Jasper's rich, slightly dramatic tones were unmistakable, but Felicity didn't recognise the other man's voice. It was deep and calm. From the corridor, she could pick out only the odd word, but from the flow of conversation, it was clear the two men had an excellent rapport.

For the briefest of moments, Felicity entertained the idea of returning later, after Jasper's visitor had left. However, their nine o'clock meeting wasn't a casual discussion between brother and sister. It was a meeting between editor and journalist, and Felicity didn't want to be late. Plus, every minute mattered with a story like Mr Reeves' murder.

She knocked on the study door and, without waiting for a response, entered the room.

Jasper was sitting comfortably, pipe in hand, in an oak and leather swivel chair behind his wide mahogany desk. He looked as dapper as ever in a dark blue suit with a red silk tie and pocket square, his glossy chestnut moustache neatly trimmed. Behind him, the windows of his study offered a broad vista of a long herbaceous border busy with bees and bathed in summer sunshine. Wise to their grandmother's disapproval of 'filling the house with the rancid stench of tobacco', Jasper had opened a window. A cool breeze scented with both floral perfume and pipe smoke flowed through the study.

"Cici." Jasper stood as Felicity entered the room, smiling at her from under his moustache. "Right on time. I'd expected nothing less. Here," he said as he rounded his desk. "Let me introduce you."

Jasper gestured towards his visitor, and the man turned in his seat. He was around Jasper's age, clean-shaven and with dark blonde swept-back hair. He wore a light grey suit with a white shirt, and as he stood up, he revealed himself to be both broad-chested and taller than Jasper. Felicity had never seen him before. She would certainly have remembered otherwise.

"This is Alexander Cooper," said Jasper. "Coop, this is my youngest sister, Lady Felicity Quick."

"Pleased to meet you, Lady Felicity," said Jasper's guest, holding out a hand.

Taking his hand, which was large and warm, and giving it the briefest of shakes, Felicity said, "Likewise, Mr Cooper," and issued a polite smile. She turned to Jasper. "Did you hear about what happened in the village?"

Jasper held up a hand. "Ho. Slow down, Cici. First thing's first. Don't you want to know what Alex is doing here?"

Felicity looked from her brother to his guest, and then back to her brother. "Yes?" she said with a quirk of her eyebrow, unconvinced that it could be more pressing than the murder story.

"Coop has just joined our paper as a news reporter. And he's not just any news reporter." Jasper slapped a hand on Alex's shoulder. "He's the very best there is."

"You're really too kind, Jasper." Alex's smile hinted at embarrassment. He cast a blue-eyed gaze towards Felicity. "We were in Ypres together. Set up the Wipers Post."

"Yes, indeed we did," said Jasper, as the two men exchanged a brief look that implied that not all their memories of the Great War were pleasant. "Interesting times they were, too."

"Congratulations on your new job, Mr Cooper," said Felicity brightly yet perfunctorily. "I also started as a news reporter for the Western Daily News just today." She turned to her brother, her smile hardening. "Remember?"

"Don't worry, Cici," said Jasper with a little laugh. "I may be a trifle older than you, but I'm not yet losing my faculties. That's actually why Alex is here. I was planning to have you shadow him for a while, so you can learn a thing or two about news reporting before we plunge you in at the deep end. Coop has an awful lot of experience. He's been on Fleet Street since the end of the war. Only now we have that awful business in the village to take into consideration, so it's a change of plan, I'm afraid."

Felicity glanced between the two men. "Shadowing? Like a trainee, you mean? I'm not starting from scratch, Jasper. I do have experience." She gave her head a shake. "Wait. You already know about the murder? How?"

Jasper tapped the side of his nose. "A good journalist never reveals his sources, Cici. You know that. And it's a bally lucky coincidence Alex is here, I can tell you. My plan was to put you on a story together, but now we've a murder on our hands, I'm putting Coop on the Reeves case right away. I'm afraid that means your start as a news reporter will be delayed, Cici."

"Delayed?" Felicity's stomach sank. "But I thought Mr Reeves' murder would be my first story."

"Your first story?" Jasper looked puzzled. "Don't worry, Cici. We'll get you trained up soon enough, but a murder isn't the right starting point for a beginner, and this story is going to be a tough nut to crack, I can tell. That's why I'm so glad Coop's here. There's no better man for the job."

Alex put his hands in his pockets. "I hope I don't let you down, Jasp. I only got in from London last night."

"But Jasper," said Felicity, desperately casting her mind back to the mental list she'd prepared of reasons she'd be good for the job. "I've lived here all my life, I have all the local connections one could possibly need, and I've already interviewed a witness. Wouldn't it make more sense if it were my story?"

A smile rippled under Jasper's moustache. "Cici. Really, now."

Felicity glared at her brother. "I'm serious, Jasper."

"Oh." Jasper's forehead creased into a frown. "Well. Sorry to let you down, old girl, but I've already given the story to Alex. Let's hope they catch the blighter who did it nice and quickly, so you can get on with shadowing Coop. If it ends up dragging on, I should be able to find someone else at the News for you to train with for a couple of months."

"A couple of months?" Felicity's mouth gaped like a fish before she came to her senses and snapped it shut. "What about my experience as a society reporter, or my work on the parish newsletter?"

"Come, now, Cici." Jasper smiled, first at Felicity, then somewhat apologetically at Alex. "I thought we discussed all this."

We didn't discuss this, Felicity wanted to say. *You told me I was going to be a news reporter. I had no idea you were making me a trainee.* Instead, she kept her thoughts to herself. She'd only just met Alex and was likely already making a terrible impression on him. But if Felicity was honest, she was not just angry at her brother. She was angry at Alex as well. By the sounds of things, he'd never even been to Lower Diddleton before, and yet here he was, claiming her story for himself.

Felicity took a deep, shaky breath. "Here's an idea," she said magnanimously. "Why don't I shadow Mr Cooper on the murder case? I'm sure I'd learn an incredible amount from him, and I'm certain my knowledge of the local area and people would be helpful."

"Tell you what, Cici," said Jasper. "Why don't you give me a moment to finish with Alex, then you and I will talk. Coop needs to get moving if he's to get a fix on the story and find a contact or two in the local police."

A flush of indignation began spreading up Felicity's neck. She looked from her brother to Alex, then back to her brother. She was at risk of saying something she would certainly later regret, so she turned on her heels and walked out of her brother's study, closing the door behind her with something of a bang.

Despite not having a specific destination in mind, Felicity strode purposefully along the corridor as a lump rose in her throat. The story she wanted to write had been given to a stranger completely unfamiliar with the local area, and Jasper found it amusing that Felicity dared suggest it should be any other way. What made it worse was that there was no one she could turn to for reassurance. Lady Henrietta did her best to be supportive, but Felicity knew whose side she'd take in this scenario, and it wouldn't be Felicity's.

Her stride slowed as she approached the end of the corridor, and she came to a stop. There, beside a marble bust on a wooden pedestal, hung a portrait of Felicity's mother in an ornate gilt frame. With her shoulders wrapped in a sumptuous fur stole, Lady Adelaide Quick had auburn curls just like Felicity's, rosy cheeks, and a twinkle in her eye. Felicity had often gazed at the portrait and wondered what her mother might think or say about a certain situation.

Taking a slow inhale, followed by a deep exhale, Felicity turned away from her mother's portrait and back towards Jasper's study. She would confront her brother about his dismissive behaviour and tell him exactly why she was the right journalist to cover the murder in—

Thwack!

Felicity walked straight into a broad chest in a light grey jacket, matching waistcoat, and crisp white shirt.

She looked up, blinking.

Staring down at her with calm, dark-blue eyes was Alex Cooper, the hint of a smile on his lips.

"Oh." said Felicity, taking a step backwards as colour rushed to her cheeks. "I'm sorry. I didn't see you there."

The hint of a smile vanished from Alex's face. "I'm the one who should apologise, Lady Felicity. I should have announced myself. It wasn't my intention to startle you."

"No, no. Not at all." Felicity smiled in a way she hoped was gracious. In Jasper's presence, she'd easily fallen into the role of little sister. Now that she and Alex were alone, it was different. Felicity usually always wanted to make a good impression, even on the man taking her story. "And please," she added. "Do call me Felicity." In her career, she was adamant she'd be known for her work and not for her station in life.

"Very well, Felicity." Alex's smile reappeared momentarily. "I came to say that Jasper's waiting for you in his study."

"Thank you," said Felicity, hoping her cheeks didn't appear as pink as they felt. "It seems my brother and I have quite a lot to talk about. We're not prone to disagreements, so I hope we haven't left you with the impression we don't get along."

"Not at all," said Alex. "Quite the opposite, in fact. Jasper clearly cares for you an awful lot. I'm certain he has your best interests at heart in recommending that you stay away from this murder business."

Felicity lifted her eyebrows, the burn of indignation returning to her chest. "I saw the victim's body myself barely an hour ago, and yet here I am without need of smelling salts or a lie-down or a warm bath. Perhaps if I donned a suit and smoked a pipe, it would help people take me more seriously. Although I must say, I fancy doing neither."

Alex scanned Felicity's face. "I see," he said, though Felicity doubted he did.

She folded her arms over her chest. "When did you arrive in Devon, Mr Cooper?"

He pushed his hands into his pockets. "Alex. Please call me Alex. I got here yesterday."

"And where are you staying? Exeter?"

He nodded. "I'm hoping to get a room at the Cat and... Cat and Custard? Is that the village inn?"

"The Cat and Cream. And had you been to Devon before arriving in the county just yesterday?"

Alex looked mildly confused. "I went to Torbay once or twice as a child. On family holidays."

"And Lower Diddleton?"

Alex frowned, his dark-blonde eyebrows drawing together to create a vertical crease at the top of his nose. "The taxi I took from Sweetbrooke station passed through Lower Diddleton on the way here, but I haven't had the pleasure of a visit yet. I'm on my way there now."

"Cici." Jasper had left the door to his study open and was making his way along the corridor. "Let's straighten things out, shall we? I've called the newsroom, and there's another reporter you can shadow. You can start your training right away."

Felicity looked from her brother to Alex, then to the portrait of her mother, who still had the rather mischievous twinkle in her eye. Before Felicity knew herself quite what she was doing, she turned with a flick of her curls and began walking confidently along the corridor, in the opposite direction of Jasper's study.

"Let's talk later, Jasper," she called over her shoulder, smiling to herself as a plan formed in her mind. "I have some rather urgent business to attend to."

Chapter Six

It was glorious weather for a motor ride. The sky was an expanse of rich blue dotted with only the occasional wisp of white cloud. Hedgerows covered with froths of scented blossom sped past as the warm summer breeze tugged at Felicity's straw cloche and whipped up Pip's blue-and-tan fur. Finnegan, the Quick family's faithful chauffeur, who was usually always at Felicity's disposal, had imagined his passengers would enjoy their journey with the roof of the dark blue Rolls-Royce lowered, and to a certain extent he was right. Pip was enjoying the breeze in his fur, but Felicity was somewhat distracted.

With her notebook balanced on her knee and her silver mechanical pencil in her hand, she was using the relatively short drive to Sittingdon Hall to get her thoughts in order. Writing things down always helped. And as she was going to write a story on the murder in Lower Diddleton — because she'd decided that was precisely what she was going to do, whether her brother or anyone else approved of it — she had to be methodical, especially if there was an extremely skilled rival already on the story. She didn't like to admit it, but Felicity's first impression of Alex was of someone exceedingly competent in anything he did.

In Pitman shorthand, which she'd learned via correspondence course and had practised enough to use at a professional speed of seventy-five words per minute, Felicity wrote the following in her notebook:

Speak to:

Witnesses who first saw the body: Mrs Winterpole (already done), Mrs Fry (the baker's wife), Mr Chesterton (landlord of the Cat & Cream), Father Neil

People who knew Mr Reeves: Lord Northcote (albeit not as a friend), Mr Reeves' maid (but will she speak to me?)

Also speak to the police: tell them about the letter in the mud, find out how the investigation is progressing

Who else to speak to?

Felicity hesitated, bringing the cool metal of the pencil to her lips. She considered rather smugly how her local contacts and knowledge put her at a distinct advantage over an out-of-towner like Alex. She knew everyone in the village, and except for the servants working in the various households, she was on speaking terms with all Lower Diddleton's inhabitants.

Then she wrote:

Local people whose names begin with N:
Father Neil
Mrs Nancy Arthur
Ned Webley
Lord Northcote

Felicity stared for a few moments at her notebook. What she'd just noted down had very little to do with writing a news article. It was more like a list of suspects, which at this stage was pure speculation, and it wasn't a journalist's business to solve the crime. Her job was to report the facts. In any case, a vicar wouldn't kill a man — that was a very basic tenet of the Christian faith — and Mrs Arthur, although spritely, was past eighty years old and walked with a cane, while Ned Webley, the butcher's boy, though tall for his age, was barely a day over fourteen. As for Lord Northcote, whether he'd fallen out with Mr Reeves or not, Felicity knew for certain her own Uncle Basil wasn't a murderer. Indeed, she was on her way to see him at precisely that moment. She would surely get a quote from him that would put the matter to rest once and for all.

Crack!

Felicity looked up, startled by the noise. Pip barked in surprise.

"There's nothing to fear, Lady Felicity," said Finnegan, without taking his eyes off the road. "Master Pip can stand down. I believe we've located Lord Northcote."

Crack!

A puff of red smoke appeared against the bright blue sky.

Finnegan slowed the motor and pulled up beside a broad wooden gate, behind a van with green and black coachwork. The view beyond the gate was of an undulating meadow dotted with buttercups. On either side of the gate was thick hedging, from beyond which came a string of oaths in Lord Northcote's impatient baritone.

"Blasted things! Let them fly again!"

Finnegan alighted from the Rolls and opened the door for Felicity.

"Thank you, Finnegan."

The driver touched his cap. "You're welcome, my lady."

"Again, I said! Again!" cried the as-yet unseen Lord Northcote.

Tucking her notebook into her pocket and assisting Pip to the ground, the Rolls' back seat being rather high for such tiny legs, Felicity set off for the wooden gate, the morning sun beating down on her shoulders.

"Come on, lads! What are you waiting for? Let it fly!"

Felicity's father, the late Lord Kingsley Quick, had been less enthusiastic about guns and hunting than the current Lord Northcote. Their friendship was mostly built upon a love of fine brandy, rare cigars, and long post-dinner conversations in the drawing rooms of Sittingdon Hall and Bradley Court. Upon the death of Felicity's father, Lord Northcote swore he would be there to support her, come what may, and insisted she could call upon him whenever needed. While wanting to interview Lord Northcote wasn't exactly a time of need, Felicity knew she wouldn't be disturbing Uncle Basil by visiting him unannounced.

"Come on, now. This is becoming exceedingly trying. Why is it taking so bally long to get the thing going again?"

Pip reached the gate before Felicity. He wriggled under it and into the meadow beyond, disappearing into a patch of tall grass. Drawing nearer to the gate, Felicity could hear an odd combination of noises, like a series of mechanical clanks followed by dinner plates being piled together.

"Sorry, my lord," came a man's voice from some distance away. "The thing kept jamming. It's ready now, my lord."

As Felicity opened the gate and stepped through, Lord Northcote came into view. He was red-cheeked, wearing his usual moss-green tweeds, and had a shotgun pressed to his shoulder, ready for aiming.

"Then what on earth are we waiting for?" he thundered from under his thick grey moustache. "Let the blasted thing fly!"

Further up the field, two of Lord Northcote's workers, both in flat caps and shirt sleeves, were huddled over some kind of contraption. With the pull of a lever and a metallic clunk, a red-brown plate flew out of the machine and into the air.

Crack! Lord Northcote let off a shot.

"Blasted thing!"

Crack! Lord Northcote's second shot met its target with a puff of red smoke against the bright blue summer sky. The smell of cordite drifted on the breeze.

"That's the ticket," said Lord Northcote, lowering his gun and watching the remains of his target fall towards the ground.

The two men at the target-firing contraption had noticed Felicity's arrival. "My lord," called one man while the other busied himself with the machine. "You've a visitor come to see you, my lord."

"What? Not again." Lord Northcote twisted towards Felicity, frowning deeply, but as soon as he saw her, his face brightened into a broad, friendly smile. "Felicity, my dear. It's you. What a pleasure." He strode towards her across the grass, his shotgun now hanging over his forearm. "And what a blessed relief. I thought it might be those wretched animal rights people again."

"Hello, Uncle Basil," said Felicity, kissing Lord Northcote on both cheeks. "What animal rights people?"

"Coombe, Mayhew." Lord Northcote shouted up the field to his men. "I've had enough for today. Pack up and let's get that blasted machine back to Sittingdon. Perhaps one of you fellows can look at it and get it working properly."

"Yes, my lord," came the response.

Lord Northcote turned to Felicity, nodding towards his workers and the contraption they were now packing away. "Been trying these blasted clay targets. Absolutely nothing like real birds, of course. Excellent shooting conditions today, as you can see. Hardly any wind, but still must have missed about a dozen of the blasted things. No more live pigeons, you see. Animal rights people saw to that. How they know to come snooping around Lower Diddleton to keep a check on things, I haven't a clue. Soon, one won't be able to ride a horse or keep a dog without someone calling it cruelty. The world has gone thoroughly mad, I tell you. Completely bally mad."

"Quite," said Felicity. Like her father, she'd never been keen on hunting, but she pondered for a moment the idea of Pip gaining access to more rights. He already wielded a great deal of influence at Bradley Court.

Having man-handled the clay target machine into its carrying box, Coombe and Mayhew positioned themselves on either side and were about to lift it when Pip approached and gave the younger of the two men's boot a good, long sniff. The workers paused their activities and glared at the little dog.

"Splendid to see you, of course, Felicity, but what brings you this way?" Lord Northcote's brow creased deeply. "There's nothing the matter with you, is there?"

"No, Uncle Basil. Nothing's wrong with me." Felicity wouldn't bring her quarrels with Jasper to Lord Northcote. "I'm absolutely fine."

The lines disappeared from Lord Northcote's forehead. "Oh, jolly good. Glad to hear it."

"As a matter of fact, I'm here to speak to you about something rather specific. Did you perhaps already hear about what happened in the village last night?"

Lord Northcote's frown reappeared. "Do you mean that nasty business on the green? Found that accountant fellow dead, didn't they? Yes, heard about that. Got the servants all atwitter. Terrible stuff. Appalling, really."

Felicity nodded. "It is rather shocking. The man they found was Mr Arthur Reeves. He was indeed a retired accountant, and I understand you knew him, Uncle Basil. I was hoping you could tell me a thing or two about him."

"Knew him? I knew the man to be a menace, but I can't say I really knew him." Lord Northcote's frowned deepened. "What's this all about, Felicity? Why do you want to know?"

"I'm writing a piece for—" Felicity hesitated "—for the parish newsletter."

It wasn't a lie, exactly. She hadn't yet handed in her resignation, and as the newsletter's editor, it was essentially up to her to decide on its contents.

"The murder will hit the village hard," she continued, "as I'm sure you can appreciate. I'd like to write something to help people make sense of what's happened."

Coombe and Mayhew at last arrived at the top of the field with the target-firing contraption in its carry box. It seemed rather heavy, and neither of the men looked particularly pleased about having to wait for Pip to finish inspecting a daisy precisely in front of the gate through which they wanted to pass.

Lord Northcote's moustache twitched. He looked at Felicity with narrowed eyes. "Very well," he said, his voice lowered so that his men couldn't hear. "I suppose I can help you with that. Have your driver bring you up to Sittingdon, Felicity. I'll tell you what you want to know about Mr Reeves."

Chapter Seven

The morning room at Sittingdon Hall was decorated with a subdued palette of soft cream and earthy beige. Low-slung armchairs with accents of polished wood sat on a deep-pile Persian rug. An elegant chaise longue with plump, velvet cushions was positioned to the side of an enormous marble fireplace. An antique Dutch vase filled with sweetly scented white lilies sat on a circular side table next to a fringed pedestal lamp.

Lady Penelope Northcote poured steaming Assam into a china cup on the side table next to Felicity's chair. Lady Northcote wore a long, drop-waist dress in pale grey with a silver sash, and her golden blonde hair had been marcelled into neat, shining waves. With her strong cheekbones and healthy complexion, she looked younger than her fifty-five years, almost girlish compared to Lord Northcote, who was a few years older than his wife.

Lord Northcote was seated opposite Felicity, his hands on the armrests of his chair. In front of the fireplace, a pouffe in the same velvet as the chaise longue's cushions had been chosen by Pip as an appropriate location for a snooze. Heather, Lady Northcote's elderly black and white Cocker Spaniel, sat to one side dejectedly, blinking sad-looking eyes and whimpering occasionally at the loss of her favourite seat.

Setting the teapot back on its tray, Lady Northcote returned to the chaise longue. She glanced at Felicity's notebook, which was open on her lap, and raised an eyebrow. "You shan't put in the parish newsletter that my husband took pleasure in the poor man's death, will you, Felicity dear?"

"I didn't say I took pleasure in the man's death, Penelope." Lord Northcote's grip tightened on the armrests of his chair. "I simply wasn't at all surprised that the infuriating fellow had irked someone to the point of not only wanting him dead but also acting on it."

"Thank you, Aunt Penelope," said Felicity, with a nod to the fresh cup of tea. "And please don't worry. I won't use Uncle Basil's more colourful remarks in the article. I want to build a picture of what kind of man Mr Reeves was, as he was not really well known in the village."

"The man said he had every right to grow the plants on his land that poisoned my horses. Had a mare almost die on me because of him. An exasperating, bloody-minded kind of man, that's what Reeves was!"

Lady Northcote sighed and shook her head. "Basil, really. There's no need to raise our voices."

Felicity continued. "I'd also like to make it clear in my article that Uncle Basil had nothing to do with the murder."

Lady Northcote twisted towards Felicity. "Why? What are people saying?"

"Would have liked to have had something to do with it," blustered Lord Northcote from under his thick moustache. "Blasted fellow."

"Basil, honestly. This is no time for such talk."

"It's quite all right," said Felicity. "There's not any real suspicion of Uncle Basil. He's well-respected in Lower Diddleton, of course, and no one locally would question his character. But the disagreement about the plants and poisoned mare is common knowledge in the village. I'd like to use my article to make it clear to everyone that there was no real enmity between Uncle Basil and Mr Reeves. There'll be people coming in from Exeter and further afield, police and press and so on—" Felicity's mind flicked to Alex. Who might he be interviewing right now? What might he be finding out about the case? "—and we don't want the wrong kind of story gathering momentum."

Lady Northcote raised her eyebrows reproachfully at her husband.

"Yes, yes. That's fair enough. I see your point, Felicity." He exhaled. "Of course I didn't kill the fellow. I didn't even wish him dead. We had our disagreement, and that was that. He made it clear to me he wouldn't change his position, so I stopped using the field. Plenty of other paddocks for my horses. Luckily, my mare pulled through, otherwise Reeves would have paid dearly."

Lady Northcote glared at her husband.

"I mean, I'd have taken it to a judge," clarified Lord Northcote. "Luckily for him, it didn't come to that."

"Do you know of anyone else locally with unpleasant experiences of Mr Reeves, Uncle Basil?"

Lord Northcote stiffened. "Not locally, no. But I'd say the man had rather a talent for upsetting people."

Felicity's pencil moved across her notepad as she spoke. "Not locally?"

"Basil..." Lady Northcote shot a glance of warning in her husband's direction.

Felicity looked from Lord Northcote to Lady Northcote. "What is it?"

"A friend of mine. Lord Harold Dalloway." Lord Northcote's voice was quieter, the bluster gone. "He knew Reeves."

"Another case of poisonous plants?" enquired Felicity.

"No. Not that." Lord Northcote gripped the armrests on his chair. "Lord Dalloway died a year or so ago, on the Buckton Park estate in Somerset. Your father knew him, too."

Lady Northcote took a sip from her teacup, which clattered a little in its saucer.

The name was familiar to Felicity, but she couldn't bring up any details. "What was Lord Dalloway's connection to Mr Reeves?"

"The story's a little complicated, and the connection with Reeves not widely known about." Lord Northcote looked at his wife. Lady Northcote closed her eyes and gave a nod. He continued. "A few years back, Lord Dalloway's accountant passed away rather suddenly. He'd been with the family for decades. Lord Dalloway sent his books to an accounting firm in Bristol and thought little of it. The firm had a solid reputation. Next thing he knew, he's getting telephone calls from the press." Lord Northcote twitched his moustache. "Journalists asking him about tax avoidance."

Felicity looked up from her notepad. "Tax avoidance?"

"You know how it is these days, Felicity," said Lady Northcote. "There's not the reverence there used to be for families like ours. Some people even delight in seeing us suffer from misfortune."

Felicity knew what Lady Northcote was saying to be true, but she'd never experienced it firsthand, and certainly not in Lower Diddleton.

Lord Northcote continued. "Lord Dalloway was tight-lipped, of course. There'd already been other peers with so-called tax irregularities dragged through the newspapers. Very embarrassing for all involved. Lord Dalloway didn't know a thing about it, anyway. So he telephoned his new accountants in Bristol to ask them what the bally hell was going on."

Lady Northcote gasped. "Basil, your language."

He continued heedlessly. "The firm said they knew nothing about it. Still, the story somehow came out. The papers didn't name Lord Dalloway, but they left enough hints to make it clear who they were talking about, and thus he was branded as a tax avoider."

"Oh, dear," said Felicity. "How dreadful."

Lord Northcote shifted in his chair, reaching into the pocket of his tweed jacket for his pipe. "Lord Dalloway had done nothing illegal, of course. His old accountant had simply made use of all the legal loopholes available for minimising one's tax bill, and Lord Dalloway never looked into the finer details of his finances himself. The poor man had done nothing wrong, in fact, but after the story appeared in the papers, everything changed. Friends started avoiding him. No one would even lift their cap to him in his local village. He was humiliated. Never recovered from it. There's no evidence he took his own life, but I believe Lord Dalloway might have remained with us longer had it not been for the whole bally tax affair."

Lord Northcote lit his pipe, puffing like a steam engine to get the thing going, smoke curling around his shoulders. Lady Northcote wrinkled her nose.

"What happened to Lord Dalloway is indeed quite terrible," said Felicity gently. "But what's the connection to Mr Reeves?"

Lord Northcote's eyes narrowed. "Reeves worked at the accountancy firm. In Bristol."

Felicity's eyes widened as she took a sip from her tea. "Our Mr Reeves?"

Lord Northcote nodded as he pulled on his pipe. "The firm denied his involvement, of course, but Reeves had left the firm of his own accord shortly after the leak to the newspapers about Lord Dalloway's finances. A mutual friend of ours looked into the matter, and it seemed rather a striking coincidence, but Lord Dalloway didn't want to press it any further."

Felicity shifted uneasily in her seat. "But why would he do it? I mean, why would Mr Reeves leak people's private financial information to the newspapers? What did he stand to gain?"

Lord Northcote shrugged. "I suppose that's simply the devilishly infuriating sort of fellow Reeves was. Some people believe they're doing a good deed for the world by having the likes of poor old Lord Dalloway labelled as a tax fraud." The bluster was returning to Lord Northcote's manner. "If you ask me, it's the same twisted logic that would drive a man to think he has a right to poison another man's horses."

There was a knock at the morning room door. The butler entered. "Telephone call for you, my lord."

Lord Northcote stared at the butler. "Is it urgent, Simmons?"

"It's your accountant, my lord."

Lord Northcote stood up rather sharply from his chair. "I'll take it. Apologies, Felicity," he said and left the room.

Felicity took another sip of her tea as she attempted to digest everything Lord Northcote had told her. It was possible Mr Reeves had more enemies than the inhabitants of Lower Diddleton may have imagined. Had Lord Dalloway still been alive, Felicity might have added him to her suspects list, although there wasn't any element of his name that could be said to start with an N. In addition, it didn't sound as though there was any proof of Mr Reeves' involvement in Lord Dalloway's disgrace.

Her thoughts were interrupted by Pip letting out a dragon-like snore, which set off Heather's whimpering.

"Heather, darling," said Lady Northcote in a tone denoting both sympathy with the dog and amusement at her melodramatic tendencies. "Do stop acting so jealously. Pip's our guest. You'll have your pouffe back when he's gone, I promise."

Felicity shared a smile with Lady Northcote. Lord and Lady Northcote had been so extremely kind to Felicity and her family over the years, especially since the passing of Felicity's father. By rights, Felicity ought to have added Lady Northcote to her list of suspects, since her name also began with an N, but the idea was ridiculous. Even if Felicity didn't know them as well as she did, Lord and Lady Northcote were too decent and upstanding to be involved in such an inhuman act as murder in the middle of the village.

But would the police take the same view?

Felicity had a duty to inform the police properly about the letter N she'd seen etched in the mud, but she also knew the detectives interviewing the villagers would hear about Mr Reeves' poisonous plants and Lord Northcote's horses. She wanted to be certain she wouldn't be putting her dear friends in danger by sharing her information with the police.

"Aunt Penelope, where were you and Uncle Basil last night?"

"Well, we had rather a lovely dinner with Colonel Lampard and his wife up at his lodge on Dartmoor. Luckily, we made it home before that awful storm started." Lady Northcote frowned a little. "Why? Oh, Felicity. You don't think—"

Felicity quickly shook her head. "No, Aunt Penelope. Of course not. But others might jump to the wrong conclusion. The disagreement between Mr Reeves and Uncle Basil is no secret."

"I see." Lady Northcote bit her lip. "Still, there's no need to worry, Felicity. We went straight to bed after arriving home from Colonel Lampard's, and I can vouch for Lord Northcote's whereabouts. I know Basil's not awfully careful about what he says, but he'll not get into any trouble. I simply won't allow it."

"I'm glad to hear that," said Felicity, a small amount of weight lifting from her chest. "And who knows? Maybe the disagreement with Uncle Basil wasn't the only quarrel Mr Reeves had locally."

Lady Northcote took a sip of tea. "Perhaps that's something you'll discover while researching your article."

Felicity nodded thoughtfully. "Indeed. Perhaps it is."

Chapter Eight

The sun was high in the cloudless sky and the church bells were striking twelve when Felicity stepped out of the Rolls and onto the pavement in front of the shops that ran alongside Lower Diddleton's village green. With her heels tapping on the grey paving stones and Pip tucked under her arm, Felicity nodded in greeting to the villagers she passed, but the street was rather empty of people. The number of police officers present on the village green, on the other hand, had increased tenfold, and with anxious groups of local onlookers gathered along the sidelines, the green looked busier than during Lower Diddleton's summer fete.

Felicity scanned the crowds for Alex, wondering if he might have already secured an interview with one of the detectives attached to the case, but reprimanded herself for becoming distracted. She had her own plan of action and would stick to it. Felicity's advantage was, after all, her local connections, and she was in the village to speak to Mrs Fry. Alongside Mrs Winterpole, Mrs Fry had been one of the first people to come across Mr Reeves' body. She might have noticed something unusual about the scene ahead of the police arriving and shooing everyone away. There was also the possibility that she knew Mr Reeves' better than most, as his passing had left her quite upset.

The bell tinkled above the door as Felicity stepped into the bakery, where it was warmer than outside in the sunshine. The walls were whitewashed, the floors were covered in gleaming white tiles, and sparkling panes of glass held up by short brass poles separated the bread, buns, and cakes from the customers. The cake counter, in particular, was a sight to behold. There were glittering maraschino cherries, bright green angelica, and sugar crystals that shone like diamonds. The rich, buttery smell of treats baking in the ovens at the back of the premises drifted through the shop, and both Felicity and Pip inhaled deeply.

Behind the counter, Mr and Mrs Fry wore aprons in brilliant white and busied themselves attending to customers. The Frys had acquired Lower Diddleton's bakery shortly after the war. The village's former baker, Mr Jenkins, only ever made cakes when customers placed special orders, but the Frys, who had come from a larger bakery in Plymouth, were more commercially minded. Besides redecorating the shop with a sleek, modern look, they expanded the bakery's offering to include all manner of sweets, including slices, tarts, and even chocolate truffles on special occasions. Old Mr Jenkins used to close his shop whenever his offering of bread ran out, which was usually half-way through the morning because he only baked one batch a day. The Frys stayed open until late afternoon, the smell of fresh bread and delicious cakes tempting villagers and passing day-trippers alike.

Felicity waited her turn in the queue while Mr and Mrs Fry chatted to customers, packaged their cakes, and rang their orders up on a large, gleaming till. Thankfully, no one entered the shop behind Felicity. At last, she found herself alone with the shop owners.

"Lady Felicity," said Mr Fry, who was just as stout as and only a little taller than his wife. "What a pleasant surprise. Surely you haven't come to fetch Bradley Court's order of scones?"

The idea of hot, buttered scones made Felicity's mouth water. "Sadly, Mr Fry, no. I haven't. I've actually come to speak to your wife."

"Me, my lady?" said Mrs Fry, bringing a plump hand to her ample bosom. She seemed fully recovered from how upset she'd been earlier. "You're very welcome to, my lady, but whatever for?"

"I'm writing an article for the parish newsletter," said Felicity, "about the terrible tragedy that befell poor Mr Reeves. It's important that everyone local is kept fully informed."

"Oh, of course, my lady. We all appreciate the parish newsletter and the work you and Father Neil put into it. We never miss an edition, do we Bernard? But as much as I'd like to be of help to you, my lady, I doubt you'll find me very useful."

"I certainly don't want to pressure you into speaking to me, Mrs Fry," said Felicity carefully. She dreaded becoming the kind of journalist that bullied people into providing statements. "But I'm certain your point of view will be a valuable addition to my article. You were among the first to come across poor Mr Reeves, were you not?"

The bell tinkled on the door as another customer entered the shop.

"Why don't you take Lady Felicity to the back kitchen, Ruth," said Mr Fry. "I'm quite capable of looking after things here without you."

"All right, Bernard. If you're sure. Come this way please, Lady Felicity."

Mrs Fry beckoned to Felicity and Pip to join her behind the counter. From there, they passed through a doorway between the bread shelves into a hot and windowless workspace flanked with ovens, worktops, and tall cooling racks. At the end was a door beyond which lay a small, neat and thankfully much cooler family kitchen. The window above the sink overlooked a tiny courtyard garden decorated with potted plants, and there was a small wooden table with two chairs. On the table lay a copy of that morning's Western Daily News. The front-page headlines announced the proposal for a new railway line in Cornwall as the most exciting news of the day, which was understandable given that the newspaper had been sent to the printer before Mr Reeves' body had been discovered.

"Do take a seat, my lady," said Mrs Fry, pulling out a chair at the table for Felicity. "Can I get you a cup of tea?"

"No, thank you," said Felicity, shifting Pip so he now sat on her lap. "I don't want to take up too much of your time. I can see that you and Mr Fry are very busy."

"If you won't have a cup of tea, then you must at least do us the honour of trying one of these." Mrs Fry brought over a tray of yellow sponge slices that had been decorated with a delicate lattice of white piping and topped with ruby-like cherries. They smelt of vanilla and cinnamon.

"It's the season for cherries, and there's plenty of them. I thought I'd try a new recipe."

"Well, Mrs Fry," said Felicity, her resistance weakening. Pip sat up on her lap and sniffed the air. "If you really must insist."

The Yorkie's twitching black nose traced the cake's journey as Felicity lifted one of the cherry slices from the tray and brought it to her mouth. The sponge was soft and airy, and the icing was as smooth as silk. The cherries were moist and dense, reminding Felicity of rich mulled wine.

"My goodness," exalted Felicity upon finishing her mouthful. "How absolutely delicious."

Mrs Fry smiled with self-satisfaction as she took the seat on the other side of the table. "Very glad you like it, my lady. Very glad indeed. Running a little shop like ours can be a lot of hard work with barely any time to rest, but it's all worth it when you see people enjoying what you've made." She dusted her hands on her apron. "Now. How can I help you with your article?"

Placing the rest of her slice on a side plate supplied by Mrs Fry, Felicity delicately wiped the crumbs from her fingertips and took her notebook and pencil from her pocket. "When you arrived on the scene with Mrs Winterpole, was there anything that stood out to you?" she asked. "Did you see anything unusual? Besides there being a dead body in the middle of our village, of course."

Mrs Fry thought for a moment, then shook her head slowly. "No, my lady. I don't think there was. But then I don't think I was looking very carefully. It got me quite upset, you see."

"Yes, of course." Felicity was a little disappointed that Mrs Fry hadn't spotted any more clues, but it was perhaps for the best that Mrs Fry hadn't noticed the N in the mud. It would be better for Lord Northcote if news about it didn't circulate around the village. "Did you know Mr Reeves well, Mrs Fry?" continued Felicity. "Is that why you were upset?"

Mrs Fry's eyebrows drew together. "I'm sorry to have given you that impression, my lady, but in all honesty, I can't say I knew the man at all. Mr Reeves visited our bakery on the odd occasion, and I knew who he was, of course, just as everyone knows who everyone is in the village. But Mr Reeves wasn't a regular customer."

"What upset you so much, then? If you don't mind me asking, of course."

Mrs Fry let her plump hands fall into her aproned lap. "It was just the shock of it, really. Someone was dead, right there on our village green. Not just dead, my lady. Murdered. It could have been anyone lying there, and I'd have had the same reaction. I feel much better than I did earlier, having had a few cups of tea and some time to come to terms with things. The vicar was very kind. But it gave me such a shock. It really did. You just don't expect to see something like that in a village like Lower Diddleton. Do you, my lady?"

"I couldn't agree more, Mrs Fry," said Felicity, making notes as she spoke. "Which is why I hope to make sense of things with my article."

"I'm sure the villagers will appreciate it, my lady. Whatever you write will be refreshing compared to what the newspapers will publish. They turn everything into a drama or a scandal. And you're certainly not the only one that's been by asking questions about Mr Reeves."

"Oh?" A pang of rivalry shot through Felicity as she imagined Alex having already coaxed information out of Mrs Fry with his smooth, deep voice. "Have there been other reporters asking to speak to you about Mr Reeves?"

"As a matter of fact, yes, my lady. Only he didn't say he was a reporter. I mean, he could have been a journalist, but I'm not sure what he was, really. And it was a couple of days ago now, at least."

Felicity raised her eyebrows. "Before Mr Reeves' death, you mean?"

"That's right," said Mrs Fry. "Funny, isn't it? Now I come to think about it. Asking me all kinds of questions, like was Mr Reeves a customer, did myself or Mr Fry ever enter into conversation with Mr Reeves about how business was at the bakery, was Mr Reeves rich. Rich, indeed! If he were, then he certainly wasn't spending it in the shops here in Lower Diddleton."

"And what were you able to tell this person asking about Mr Reeves?"

"Hardly anything, my lady. In all honesty, I didn't know the answers to half the man's questions. Even if I had known, I wouldn't have said anything. I asked the gentleman why he wanted to know so much about Mr Reeves, and the answer he gave was rather vague. Said he had business with him and wouldn't say more than that. In the end, I politely suggested that he put his questions to Mr Reeves himself. He was alive at the time, of course, poor soul."

"Did the man give you his name?"

"Mac-something. I don't fully remember. He was Scottish, my lady."

"What did he look like?"

Mrs Fry considered the question for a moment. "He was an older gentleman. Very presentable. Had a rather fancy moustache. Do you know what he said to me? He said should I change my mind about knowing anything about Mr Reeves, then I could ask for him at the Cat and Cream. Really, my lady. Have you ever heard anything more ridiculous? How could I change my mind about knowing something? You either know something, or you don't."

"You're quite right, Mrs Fry," said Felicity thoughtfully, for Mrs Fry had provided more useful information than the interviewee herself might have realised.

"Will you be attending the memorial service, my lady? It'll be held first thing tomorrow morning in the church. The vicar said it'll be a chance for the village to gather not only to pay their respects but to support one another."

"Yes, Mrs Fry. I believe I will." Felicity narrowed her eyes, deep in thought. "But first, I think I'll pay a visit to the Cat and Cream."

Chapter Nine

Felicity walked briskly along the village high street, placing Pip on the pavement so he could trot alongside her. Before leaving the bakery, Mrs Fry had insisted on giving Pip one of the biscuits she baked especially for the dogs that visit her shop. Felicity didn't have time to attend to it now, but Pip had crumbs in the fur under his chin. She'd give him a good brush later on.

As the heels of her T-bar shoes clicked along the pavement, Felicity's stomach squeezed with a rush of what could only be described as excitement. What if Lower Diddleton's parish newsletter scooped the Western Daily News, uncovering the secrets of Mr Reeves' life and the reason he'd been killed before the newspapers even got a whiff of it? That would certainly teach Jasper to have more faith in her. And it would also show Alex that he couldn't arrive in a village he'd never set foot in before and claim the biggest story ever to happen in its history. Indeed, the whole thing felt rather fortuitous. Had Felicity been given the opportunity to resign from her position on the parish newsletter, she'd now have nowhere to publish her story on the murder.

But upon scanning the activity on the village green, Felicity's heart fell a little. Among the legions of police and auxiliary workers that with their boots and vehicle tyres were turning the grass into a quagmire of red mud, Felicity spotted the tall, broad-shouldered frame and dark blond hair of Alex. He stood close to the duck pond, the body of Mr Reeves now removed from the site, and was in deep conversation with a man in a long grey overcoat and brown Homburg hat. It had to be a police detective, and Alex was making copious notes as the detective spoke. Their faces were serious, but their manner one of professional camaraderie.

Felicity had never interviewed a police detective before. She wouldn't know how to go about it. She knew, however, that she needed to speak to the police, if only to report what she'd seen at the crime scene, but she wasn't looking forward to sharing news of a clue that pointed towards her Uncle Basil. If only there was evidence pointing elsewhere, too.

That was partly why she was on her way to the Cat and Cream. Who was the man who'd been asking questions about Mr Reeves prior to his death? And what had been his interest in Mr Reeves?

The Cat and Cream Inn, the origins of its name lost to history, had been at the centre of Lower Diddleton since medieval times. It was once an important staging post on the main coaching route between Plymouth and Exeter that ran across the moors. Now, it was a destination for villagers and visitors alike, serving not only as a meeting location for locals but also as a place where tourists could eat a hearty meal and find a bed for the night.

The front of the inn was festooned with hanging baskets and window boxes full of flowers in bright pinks, reds, and yellows, but the building itself had changed little since its days as a coaching inn. It still had a cobbled courtyard around which the horses used to be stabled and which was now full of wooden chairs and tables, each decorated with a potted plant. To the delight of day-trippers arriving in charabancs with their Brownie cameras at the ready, the roof of the inn was thatched in combed wheat reed, as per the local tradition. It made the building appear to have a thick head of neatly trimmed blond hair.

In another twist of good luck, the landlord, Mr Chesterton, was outside the Cat and Cream, contorting his wiry frame over a chalkboard sign. In bright red, he crossed out *VACANCIES* and wrote next to it: *FULL,* his bald patch glinting in the sun as he worked.

"Mr Chesterton," said Felicity. "You're just the man I was hoping to see."

The landlord straightened himself and turned towards her, giving her a limp smile. "Lady Felicity, what a pleasant surprise," he said flatly. "What brings you to the Cat and Cream? Will you be joining us for lunch? If so, then I recommend you place your order with my staff right away. We're quite busy, as I'm sure you can appreciate, what with all the goings-on in the village. Got rather a large number of policemen—" he enunciated the word carefully, as though speaking to someone hard of hearing "—booked in for the night. From the detective branch at Exeter, most of them."

Aware that business-minded men like Mr Chesterton preferred not to waste time on trivial matters, Felicity spoke rather bluntly. "Thank you for the invitation to lunch, but I was hoping to have a few minutes of your time, Mr Chesterton. I'm writing an article for the parish newsletter about the murder, and I have a few questions I'm sure you'll be able to help me with."

Pip sniffed at Mr Chesterton's shoe, but the landlord didn't seem to notice. "Is that so?" he said, stroking his thin moustache. "And do you need these few minutes of my time urgently, or can it wait until later in the afternoon, once lunch has been served?"

Felicity thought for a moment. The parish newsletter had a rather unpredictable publishing rhythm. At a minimum, there was a newsletter every month, but there could be extra editions for special events like the summer fete or unpredictable developments like when the giant oak at the northwest corner of the village green had to be felled after being damaged in a spring storm.

While not a development with perhaps as many practical implications for Lower Diddleton as the felling of the mighty oak — which resulted in the high street being closed to traffic for two days — Felicity saw the murder of Mr Reeves as an event worthy of a special edition, and not only because of her wild dream of scooping her brother's newspaper. The murder was such a highly unusual and shocking event, it warranted the extra attention. The deadline would be tight, but Felicity was confident she could put an edition together for publication tomorrow. After completing as many interviews as possible, she would spend the evening and most likely much of the night writing up her copy, with a view to distributing prints of the newsletter in the village the following day.

"Well, Mr Chesterton, I should like to get this edition to the printer early tomorrow morning, so I—"

"Then you won't mind if we speak later, will you, Lady Felicity? The policemen who've just taken up my remaining rooms all need feeding. I've ordered extra sausages and bacon from the butcher for breakfast tomorrow, of course. Then there'll be the inquest in a couple of days, which will take place here, at the Cat and Cream, seeing as it's the most suitable venue." The landlord couldn't hide his satisfaction with this last piece of information, his barely hidden smile rather inappropriate given that a brutal murder was the reason for his inn's good fortune.

Felicity frowned. "As I was about to say, Mr Chesterton, I won't take up much of your time at all. I have a question about one of your guests, and I should be pleased if—"

"Aha. Gentlemen." Mr Chesterton's eyebrows lifted as his gaze shifted away from Felicity. "Come for lunch, have you? I've put on a special menu for you all today. Got to keep our Bobbies well fed, haven't we?"

Felicity turned to see Sergeant Hodgkins and Constable Price standing behind her, their faces, one round and the other thin, severe under their helmets.

"No, thank you, Mr Chesterton," said the sergeant brusquely. "There's no time for luncheon. We're here on police business. We need to speak to Lady Felicity."

Chapter Ten

Mr Chesterton having disappeared into the Cat and Cream mumbling something about lunch bookings and table settings, Felicity found herself alone in the inn's courtyard with the two policemen. Their dark blue uniforms, shining silver buttons and badges, and grave expressions put Felicity on edge, even though she was guilty of precisely nothing.

She scooped Pip up and tucked him under her arm. "Sergeant Hodgkins, Constable Price. How may I be of assistance to you?"

Sergeant Hodgkins tucked his thumbs into the black leather belt encircling his rather generous waist and lowered his eyebrows. "We've spent quite a bit of our valuable time looking for you this morning, Lady Felicity. Been to Bradley Court, then up to Sittingdon Hall. Missed you on every occasion. We thought maybe you'd left the country till Constable Price here spotted you from across the green."

The lanky constable could barely suppress a look of pride at this achievement as he stood obediently beside his superior, his hands clasped behind his back.

Felicity's cheeks flushed a little. Being in trouble was rarely enjoyable. "I wasn't aware I was under house arrest, Sergeant Hodgkins."

The sergeant sighed irritably. "No one's placed you under arrest yet, Lady Felicity. You know that. But we told you we'd be looking to speak with you about the incident with Mr Reeves, didn't we?"

"Indeed, you did," said Felicity. "However, I don't remember receiving any instructions on how our meeting was to happen, and what, may I ask, do you mean by no one having 'yet' placed me under arrest? Am I a suspect?" If her own name had made it onto the police's list, then their investigation was going even worse than she'd imagined.

It was Constable Price's turn to say something. "It's early days yet, my lady." His voice was deep and slow. "All avenues of investigation are still open."

Sergeant Hodgkins nodded with satisfaction. "That's right. Can't rule anything out at this stage."

"Well, perhaps I can assist in that regard," said Felicity. She wasn't keen on doing it, but she had to present her evidence to the police at some point, and if she waited any longer to do so, she may well find herself in real trouble with the law. She cleared her throat. "I saw something I'm sure you'll find very interesting."

Sergeant Hodgkins held up a hand. "Yes, my lady, I'm sure you did, but there is a process that must be followed. If you don't mind." He gestured towards a seat at one of the courtyard's tables.

Felicity smiled tightly as she took a seat, placing Pip on her lap. His little body felt tense, and Felicity wasn't enjoying herself either.

Sergeant Hodgkins took a seat on the opposite side of the little round table while Constable Price remained standing at his elbow. In the middle of the table stood a terracotta pot with a bright red geranium in it. The sergeant scowled at the pot. He switched his glare to his subordinate, then back to the plant. Constable Price dutifully stepped forward and removed the potted monstrosity, setting it down on another of the courtyard's tables. Sergeant Hodgkins gave a curt nod of satisfaction.

"Now," said the sergeant as he pulled a small, spiral-bound notebook from the top pocket of his jacket. Licking the tips of his fingers, he flicked to the correct page. His eyes scanned what was written there, then he looked at Felicity. "When did you come across the body of Mr Reeves?"

Felicity blinked. "Not long before you and Constable Price arrived on the scene. I was there after Mrs Winterpole, Mrs Fry, Mr Chesterton, and Father Neil."

Sergeant Hodgkins made notes, paused, then looked up at Felicity. "What did you see or hear prior to coming across the victim's body that might be relevant to Mr Reeves' death?"

"Why, nothing whatever," said Felicity without hesitation. "I'd come across our kitchen maid on the lane into Lower Diddleton. She mentioned there was some kind of gathering on the village green, but she said nothing about there having been a murder, and naturally, I imagined nothing of the sort to have happened."

The sergeant continued his note-taking for a moment. "What's the name of your kitchen maid, Lady Felicity?"

"Janey Whedon, but there's no need to go bothering her. I don't see what she's got to do with anything."

"I believe that's for the police to decide, my lady," said Sergeant Hodgkins matter-of-factly. Again, he checked his notebook. "So, what you're telling us is that you know nothing that could be of any use to us in our investigations?"

"I'm sorry, Sergeant Hodgkins," said Lady Felicity patiently, "but I don't believe that's what I said."

"Aha. So you know something, after all."

Felicity nodded and stroked Pip's head. "As I tried telling you earlier, I noticed something at the scene of the crime."

"Very good, my lady," said Sergeant Hodgkins, resuming his note-taking. "What was it you saw?"

"Well," she began, repositioning Pip on her lap. "As I saw it, Mr Reeves was lying face-down in the mud."

"That's correct."

"With a hand outstretched by his face."

"Also correct."

"And next to his hand, in the mud, he'd used his last moments to write something."

"Write something?"

"Yes. He'd written the letter N."

Sergeant Hodgkins frowned, his chin pressed into the flesh of his neck. "The letter N?"

Felicity nodded. "Yes. He'd written the letter N in the mud. With his finger."

The sergeant looked at Constable Price, who was also frowning. "When we searched the scene, constable, did we come across any letters written in any mud?"

"No, sir. We didn't."

"And we searched the scene thoroughly, did we not?"

"We did, sir, yes."

Sergeant Hodgkins turned back to Felicity. "I'm sorry, my lady. While I don't wish to accuse you of lying, what you've told us can't be true. We carried out a thorough search of the scene and found no such evidence. You must be mistaken."

Felicity cleared her throat a little, aware of the delicacy of the matter. "I quite understand your confusion, Sergeant Hodgkins, and that of Constable Price. The reason you found nothing would be because shortly after I saw the letter in the mud, all trace of it was destroyed."

"Destroyed?" Sergeant Hodgkins' eyes widened dramatically. "How? By who?"

"Well, by Constable Price. He stood on it."

The sergeant fired an angry glance at his subordinate. The young constable's face was blameless, of course, as he had no idea of what he'd done, and he shrugged and shook his head at his superior, who then turned his angry gaze back on Felicity. "And why, Lady Felicity, would Constable Price destroy a piece of evidence?"

"I don't believe he did it deliberately," said Felicity plainly. "I would say that it was done through clumsiness and a lack of experience in preserving crime scenes."

The sergeant's jowls flushed red. "And why, Lady Felicity, did you not tell us about this supposedly vital piece of evidence earlier this morning?"

"I tried, Sergeant Hodgkins. Really, I did. But you insisted we should talk later."

The rotund policeman huffed out of his nose like a furious bull. "As I said, I don't wish to accuse anyone of being a liar, but I find it hard to believe that my constable, a trained officer of the law, would be capable of such a blunder. What evidence do you have of there ever having been anything written in the mud, Lady Felicity? Did anyone else see this supposed letter N?"

"I don't think so," said Felicity. "The only proof I have is that I saw it with my own eyes."

Sergeant Hodgkins scoffed dismissively. "Then your eyes must have deceived you." He stuffed his notepad back into his top pocket and stood up. "I think we've heard quite enough of your testimony, Lady Felicity. Thank you for your time. Good day."

The sergeant left the inn courtyard, Constable Price close behind him, their boots clattering on the cobblestones. The abruptness of their departure was a little bewildering.

"I'm not sure they believed me, Pip," said Felicity as she stroked the Yorkie's head. "But I know what I saw. You saw it too, didn't you?"

The little dog gave a yap of assent.

"Exactly," she said as she set Pip on the ground and he went back to sniffing under the tables for any fallen food the sparrows hadn't yet found. "But I've at least done my best to tell the police. Perhaps it's better for Uncle Basil that they don't believe me."

Standing up, Felicity collected the potted geranium Constable Price had moved to another table and set it back in its rightful position.

"You shouldn't give up on your dreams so easily."

Felicity turned.

Alex Cooper was standing at the entrance to the inn's courtyard, his hands in his pockets and a smile on his face.

Chapter Eleven

How long had Alex been standing there watching her? Had he heard her talking to herself. To Felicity's extreme dismay, colour began rising in her cheeks.

"I'm sorry, I don't quite follow." She shook her head, her curls dancing by her ears. "Exactly how am I 'giving up on my dreams'?"

Pip went on the defensive, standing next to Felicity's ankles and growling at Alex. Usually she'd have chastised the Yorkie, but Alex was the last person on Earth she felt like speaking to right now, and it really wasn't done to sneak up on a person like that.

Advancing into the courtyard, Alex's dark blue eyes scanned the neatly arranged tables with their potted plants. He stopped a short distance from Felicity, and his gaze settled calmly upon her.

"From what Jasper's told me, working at an inn would be a very sad waste of your talents."

"If you've come here to mock me," Felicity said coolly, "may I kindly request that you save it for another occasion because to be frank with you, I'm simply not in the mood for it."

Alex frowned, surprised. "Clearly, I overestimate my comedic abilities. My apologies. I intended no offence."

The colour receded a little from Felicity's face. "Pip, please," she said, but the Yorkshire Terrier continued to growl.

"That's all right," said Alex with a nod towards Pip. "I suppose I'm more of a cat person, and perhaps he senses that. Say, I understand you're writing a piece for the village newsletter about the murder. Is that right?"

"The parish newsletter," Felicity corrected flatly, although it never failed to surprise her how quickly news travelled in Lower Diddleton. "The newsletter covers the hamlets of Ashstone, Oakridge Head, and Venny Upton, in addition to the village of Lower Diddleton. And that is right. I'm writing an article about the murder."

"Have you got very far with your research?"

"You could say that, yes." *Further than the local police, by the sound of things*, but Felicity kept her misgivings about the sergeant and constable to herself. "And you? Have you made progress even without the benefit of local contacts?"

Alex nodded. "It's not going too badly." He withdrew a hand from his pocket and swept it over his hair. Felicity noticed a pale scar on his forehead, which dipped to the corner of his eye. A war wound, perhaps.

"What have you found out?" asked Felicity.

Alex exhaled. "Not an awful lot so far. The police don't have any firm suspects yet." Felicity was relieved to hear no mention of Lord Northcote. "And hardly anyone locally seems to know the first thing about Mr Reeves. I've been hoping to speak to his maid, but the police have kept her rather busy with their interviews. Got any idea who else I might speak to?"

Felicity smiled and shook her head. "I'm afraid not." It felt oddly good to be considered someone Alex might want to glean information from, but she wasn't naïve enough to give away her leads. "There's indeed not much to the story at this stage, is there?"

Alex nodded thoughtfully. "Listen," he said, his gaze now serious. "I know it might not seem like it with so many police officers around, but reporting on a murder can be a dangerous business."

Pip growled with renewed vigour. Felicity scooped the little dog into her arms, but he wouldn't be placated. Indeed, Felicity was herself quite tired of hearing what other people thought best for her.

"Well, thank you for the advice," she said, "but I really must get along." With Pip still under her arm, Felicity started towards the village high street. "I have a story to write, as I know you do, too."

As she passed him, Alex briefly put a hand on Felicity's elbow. The surprise of his touch brought her to an abrupt standstill. Pip continued to growl.

"What's your angle?" Alex asked.

"M-my angle?"

"What angle have you chosen for your story?"

"Oh," said Felicity, shaking her head a little. "I'm writing about the effect of the murder on the village."

"Good. Leave it at that."

"What do you mean?"

"Stay away from the investigation. Leave it to the police."

Alex's eyes were clear and honest, and his concern for her seemed genuine, but Felicity didn't need anyone else to protect her from being a news reporter. She had Jasper and Lady Henrietta for that.

"I know how to take care of myself," she said, "and I have a story to write. Good day to you."

Without looking back, and with Pip still growling under her elbow, Felicity strode out of the inn's courtyard and onto the village high street with an air of confidence. Inside, however, she felt very differently indeed.

As large white clouds scudded across the sky and threatened to blot out the sun, Felicity walked home to Bradley Court as quickly as she could. The encounter with Alex had rattled her, though she couldn't exactly say why. He'd got under her skin somehow. Pip trotted beside Felicity for a short while, but by the time they passed the cherry orchard, he was asking to be picked up again. Felicity was walking too fast for him.

An interview with the Cat and Cream's landlord was still on

Felicity's list of things to accomplish. She also ought to at least inform the vicar about the extra edition of the parish newsletter, although Father Neil would likely be fully occupied preparing the memorial service. Still, Felicity had given into the urge to escape the village. Lower Diddleton was noisier and busier than usual with so many police officers about, and she didn't like the idea of Alex watching her every move. Besides, there was plenty she could get done from Bradley Court. The telephone was an exceedingly useful device.

Cutting through Bradley Court's formal gardens, Felicity spotted her grandmother. Lady Henrietta was at the back of a deep herbaceous border, doing battle with a towering clump of unruly hollyhocks, which had flowered in shades of plum, pink, and white.

"Hello, Grandmama." Felicity waved, but kept moving.

"Oh, Felicity." Lady Henrietta straightened, her hands still busy with string and canes. "Good that you're back. Jasper was looking for you. He's in his study. Will you see him?"

"Certainly," called Felicity as she continued towards the terrace, and it wasn't a lie, but it also wasn't something she planned on doing that same day.

Lady Henrietta turned to follow Felicity's progress through the garden, but she couldn't let go of the twine already wrapped around the hollyhocks. "You've missed lunch, you know. You need to eat, dear. Have Cook make you a sandwich. You'll do that, won't you?"

"Of course, Grandmama," said Felicity, who didn't feel hungry at all and had much more important things to worry about than lunch.

Once indoors, Felicity went to the telephone table, which was tucked into a nook next to the boot room in the main entrance hall. Given that Jasper was home, it wasn't ideal to be discussing her plans where anyone passing could hear, but what choice did she have? The only other telephone at Bradley Court was in Jasper's study. While Pip took a long drink from a water bowl positioned between the feet of a full suit of armour bearing the Quick family pennant, Felicity lifted the telephone receiver and asked the operator to connect her to Mr Duggan, the printer in Sweetbrooke.

"Terrible business, isn't it, my lady?" said Mr Duggan, the rhythmic workings of his Linotype printing press audible in the background. "The poor fellow, killed like that in the middle of the village. Quite understandable that you want to publish a special edition. You'd like to get it out by tomorrow, you say?"

"Precisely," said Felicity. "I'll attend the memorial service at the church before turning in my copy, as I'd like to include a report of the service in the newsletter."

"If you get everything to me by midday, my lady, we'll be able to deliver the prints to Lower Diddleton the same evening. I can imagine the vicar is quite keen to use the newsletter to reassure everyone."

"Quite," said Felicity somewhat awkwardly, for she'd yet to discuss the matter of a special edition with Father Neil, though it was certainly on her to-do list. "Thank you, Mr Duggan."

After finishing her call with the printer, Felicity picked up the receiver and dialled again. The vicar wasn't at the rectory, but his housekeeper made a note about the special edition and promised to inform Father Neil when he came home for dinner.

Again Felicity picked up the telephone receiver, this time asking to be connected to the Cat and Cream. As the operator put her through, she drummed her fingers on the telephone desk. Would she have the good fortune to get all her telephoning done without being interrupted by Jasper?

"Good afternoon," said a cheery young man. "This is the Cat and Cream Inn at Lower Diddleton. How may I help you?"

"I'd like to speak to Mr Chesterton, please." It was approaching two o'clock. The mad rush for lunch was surely over by now.

"Certainly. Who shall I say is asking after him?"

"Lady Felicity Quick."

"Just one moment, my lady."

The other end of the line went quiet. Pip's paws clicked on the entrance hall floor as he approached Felicity to express interest in sitting on her lap.

"Lady Felicity?" The clerk at the inn was back on the line.

"Yes?" answered Felicity, scooping Pip onto her lap with her free hand.

"I'm afraid Mr Chesterton's unavailable. Can I take a message?"

Felicity sighed. "No, thank you." Then she had a thought. "But you might help me with something else."

"Certainly, my lady. I'm at your disposal."

"Do you have a Scottish guest staying at the inn? His name is Mac-something, I believe."

"Allow me just one moment, my lady, while I check our guest book. We don't have many visitors all the way from Scotland." Pages were turned. "Hmm. Not that I can see, no. Ah, sorry. Yes. We have a Mr Alistair McNabb staying with us. Is that who you perhaps meant, my lady?"

Felicity swallowed. The name didn't exactly start with an N, but it wasn't far off.

"Is he indeed a Scotsman?"

"It says here that his normal residence is in Edinburgh."

"And does he have a rather distinctive moustache?"

"I couldn't say, my lady. I don't believe I've seen him myself. He must have been checked in by one of the other clerks."

Still, it had to be the man Mrs Fry had spoken about. As the clerk himself said, visitors from Scotland weren't common in Lower Diddleton.

"Until when is Mr McNabb staying at the inn?"

"He has another night with us, my lady."

"Thank you. You've been incredibly helpful."

Replacing the receiver, Felicity exhaled and stroked a hand over Pip's silky fur. The obvious thing would be to set up a meeting with Mr McNabb, ask him what his business had been with Mr Reeves, and find out what he knew about the murder victim. That's probably what a real news reporter would do. But what if Mr McNabb had something to do with Mr Reeves' death? Was this what Jasper and Alex had meant about murder being a dangerous business? The last thing Felicity wanted to do was to get herself in trouble and prove them right.

Footsteps echoed in the hallway, and Pip's ears pricked up. Felicity braced herself for another confrontation with Jasper, so when Lady Henrietta appeared before the telephone nook, her garden hat in her hand, her grey curls wrapped into an elegant chignon at the back of her head, Felicity sighed with relief.

"Have you eaten yet, dear?"

"Not yet, Grandmama."

Lady Henrietta closed her eyes for a moment in a silent prayer for the strength to deal with her wayward granddaughter. "Will you be here for dinner at least?"

Felicity glanced at the grandfather clock. It was just after two. She had a lot of work ahead of her if she was to get everything to the printer by noon the next day, and she desperately hoped she had enough ribbons for her typewriter, which sat waiting for her like a faithful friend upstairs on the rosewood desk before her bedroom window.

"Will Jasper be present at dinner?"

"No, dear. He'll be in Bristol for meetings with the newspaper's advertisers."

Thank goodness, thought Felicity, careful not to allow her relief to show.

"Did you speak to him yet?" urged Lady Henrietta.

"Not yet," said Felicity. "I'll stay for dinner. But first—" she stood up from the telephone table, scooping Pip under her arm "—I've work to do."

Leaving her grandmother sighing in the hall, a plan crystallised in Felicity's mind as she ascended the broad, carpeted stairs to Bradley Court's first floor. She'd type and edit everything she could that afternoon — the interviews with Mrs Winterpole and Mrs Fry, a quote from Lord Northcote about his dismay at the deceased's passing, and her own impressions of how the murder had brought disruption and distress to the village. Then, in the morning, she would attend the memorial service. If Mr McNabb, the Scotsman with a distinctive moustache, was at the service, Felicity would approach him and put her questions to him. For what danger could there be in a church full of people?

But if Mr McNabb wasn't at the memorial service, then Felicity would let it go. It wasn't her job to solve the case. It was her job to keep the parishioners informed, and she wasn't quite as naïve as Alex and Jasper thought she was. She knew how to stay out of harm's way, and she knew how to put a parish newsletter together at short notice, which was exactly what she would do.

Chapter Twelve

ALL ANGELS CHURCH, LOWER DIDDLETON, EAST DEVON, 12 JUNE 1921

Felicity's plan was ticking along like clockwork. She'd typed up all the interviews, information, and impressions she'd gathered so far for the special edition of the parish newsletter. She'd avoided her brother, dining in relative peace with Lady Henrietta, and she'd even had a restful night's sleep. With rain falling softly onto black umbrellas in the churchyard of All Angels, Felicity and her grandmother were now joining the queue of people waiting to enter the church for Mr Reeves' memorial service, which started at nine o'clock. Felicity still intended to speak to Mr Chesterton, who'd remained unreachable by telephone even after several attempts, but she was confident she'd see him at the memorial service, although there was as yet no sign of either the inn landlord or the mysterious Scotsman, Mr McNabb.

The smell of wet grass rose from between the headstones, a single bell tolled mournfully, and the queue taking up the length of the churchyard's gravel path shuffled slowly forwards. Felicity and her grandmother were the only members of the Quick family in attendance, Jasper still being caught up in meetings in Bristol, and Pip having been left at Bradley Court as he couldn't be trusted not to snore during the service.

"I'm rather stunned the man was so popular," whispered Lady Henrietta, craning her neck to peer out from under the umbrella at the long line of people ahead. Under a fur-edged cape, she wore a high-collared dress trimmed with delicate lace, all of it black. "It's busier than midnight mass on Christmas Eve."

"Quite." Felicity had chosen to wear an unadorned dropped-waist dress in black crepe, a raincoat in rubberised black cotton, and a black toque that pressed her auburn curls to her cheeks. Like her grandmother, she scanned the gathering, only she wasn't marvelling at the crowds. She was looking for the gentleman with the 'fancy' moustache. "I suppose people tend to come together at times of crisis".

"Lady Henrietta, Lady Felicity." Mrs Winterpole joined the queue behind them. She wore a dark grey coat and a wide-brimmed black hat. "I was about to say how lovely it is to see you both, but it's rather a sad business bringing us together this morning, isn't it?"

"My sentiments exactly, Mrs Winterpole," replied Felicity's grandmother without a hint of animosity, which was unusual given that the two women could clash rather fiercely at various local committees on topics as controversial as the type of hydrangea that should be planted in dry shade. "What happened to poor Mr Reeves is abhorrent. I can't say I ever agreed with any of the suggestions he offered for our village's flowerbeds, but I certainly never wished the man any ill. Felicity told me you were the first to come across the body, Mrs Winterpole. I can only imagine what a terrible shock that must have been."

"It was indeed rather awful," said Mrs Winterpole with a solemn shake of her head. "But to add insult to injury, have you seen what those careless police officers have done to our village green? All those motors churning up the ground with their tyres. It's become a mud bath. The green is absolutely ruined."

As Lady Henrietta and Mrs Winterpole commiserated one another on the lack of respect shown for the hours of hard work that went into keeping the grass on the village green in good condition,

Felicity subtly stepped away from the churchyard queue and scanned the village high street for any sign of Mr Chesterton or Mr McNabb. Her mind went also to Alex. Would he attend the memorial service? It was more for local people and those who knew Mr Reeves personally than an occasion for the press. Even the police had agreed not to attend, though they had insisted on stationing some uniformed officers near the church.

With the queue now moving, Felicity rejoined Lady Henrietta and Mrs Winterpole as they passed through thick oak doors and into the church's vestibule, where umbrellas could be closed. In the nave beyond, the rows of wooden pews were almost full. Given that Mr Reeves hadn't made many or perhaps any friends in the village during his residency, there was an obvious need among local people to come together for reassurance in the face of tragedy. Felicity hoped her special edition of the newsletter would help in that regard.

Entering the nave, Felicity scanned the crowd, but there was hardly a face she didn't recognise. There was Mrs Broughton and her husband, both looking rather stern and sad, Mr and Mrs Fry, who appeared distinctly less jolly than usual and quite different without their white aprons, and the butcher and his wife, who rarely smiled anyway and who had also changed out of their usual white coats. The only person Felicity couldn't put a name to was a young girl with bobbed brown hair and delicate features who sat weeping on the front pew. Her narrow shoulders shook as she dabbed at her eyes with a simple white handkerchief.

Finding a seat towards the back of the church, those already seated squeezing further along the pew to make room for the Quicks and Mrs Winterpole, Felicity whispered to her grandmother. "Who's the young woman at the front? She seems terribly upset. Do you suppose she's a relative of Mr Reeves?"

Lady Henrietta shifted in her seat to find a comfortable position on the hard, cramped pew, and squinted through the rows of people. "Oh, yes, dear. I see her. But do you know, I'm actually not quite sure who she is."

Mrs Winterpole, who was seated on the other side of Lady Henrietta, leaned in. “That’s Nora Andrews. She was Mr Reeves’ maid, and it’s no wonder the poor thing’s so upset. She worked for him for less than a year, and I gather it was her first position as a domestic. His death must have been a very nasty shock for her.”

Nora Andrews. It was a name that began with the letter N, but could such a young, fragile-looking girl be capable of shooting someone dead? And then, having done so, attend her victim’s memorial service the next day in a state of deep distress? Felicity supposed it wasn’t impossible, but the chances seemed remote. Plus, as a domestic, Nora would surely have been able to do away with Mr Reeves without needing to leave his body in the middle of the village for everyone to find. The police had also doubtlessly already spoken to Nora at length, although that somehow wasn’t as reassuring as it should have been.

An interview with the dead man’s maid would be an interesting addition to the parish newsletter, but Felicity decided she would only attempt to speak to Nora when the poor girl was less upset. She didn’t want to intrude on anyone’s grief. Besides, time was ticking to meet the midday deadline the printer had given her, and Felicity still needed to write up the memorial service and anything she could glean from Mr Chesterton or Mr McNabb, if she found the chance to speak to them. There would always be future editions of the newsletter in which further interviews could feature.

As the mournful bell slowed its tolling, Felicity twisted in her seat to look at the late-comers. Lord and Lady Northcote weren’t in attendance, but the two gamekeepers from the clay pigeon shoot, Coombe and Mayhew, were present. They stood against the back wall of the nave, their caps in their hands, both of them looking rather uncomfortable. Had they been ordered to attend, or were they there of their own accord? As the younger of the two gamekeepers turned his gaze upon her, Felicity smiled politely and looked away, only for her eyes to settle on a sight that made her stomach squeeze.

Further along the back wall, next to an ornate marble memorial,

Alex stood gazing out across the packed pews. He wore a navy suit with a dark grey tie and had his notebook in his hand. What was he doing here? Felicity was still rather vexed about her encounter with him the day before. She'd also seen an article about the murder with Alex's byline in the newspaper that very morning. It didn't contain many details. It simply announced that the murder had taken place and that the investigation was underway, which was likely all that could be submitted ahead of the printing deadline. She wondered what his write-up of the memorial service would be like. How would hers compare? Surely, she'd have the upper hand, knowing the village as well as she did, but perhaps Alex's outsider status would allow him to notice things Felicity might not. Although, as an outsider, it was debatable whether he should be at the memorial service at all. There were no other journalists present. Was Alex the ruthless sort?

Alex's gaze landed on Felicity, and he smiled. She gave a prim nod of acknowledgment and turned back to face the front of the church, heat rising in her cheeks. Considering they were professional rivals, Alex's manner was unusually amiable. Or was he mocking her?

Father Neil, clearing his throat, took his place in the pulpit in front of the ancient wooden rood screen, prompting the church to become suddenly very quiet. The soft closing of the doors at the side of the nave drew Felicity's attention. An older man of refined appearance in a high-collared jacket stood beside the door, his arms folded over his chest. As the man cast a glance across the crowded pews, Felicity saw that his grey moustache was waxed upwards into curls at the ends. It had to be Mr McNabb, and Felicity already had her first clue about his relationship with Mr Reeves, because he didn't look very upset. He looked rather peeved.

When the vicar began his address, his face was both serene and sorrowful. "Mr Arthur Reeves hadn't been part of our parish for very long, but whether or not Mr Reeves was well known to you, the deeply sad and sudden way in which his life ended here in our normally peaceful village has touched every one of us gathered today."

Felicity took notes throughout the service, but Father Neil had little to share in the way of details about Mr Reeves' life. No relatives were called upon to speak, and the facts the vicar had on the dead man were mostly ones Felicity already knew. Mr Reeves had worked as an accountant and had lived in Bristol before relocating to Lower Diddleton, where he devoted himself to his garden and love of exotic plants. The vicar also mentioned Mr Reeves' service during the war, saying he'd served as a Quartermaster-Sergeant in the Somerset Light Infantry, seeing action on both the Western Front and in Mesopotamia.

Throughout the service, Felicity glanced surreptitiously at Mr McNabb. While some members of the congregation dabbed at their eyes with handkerchiefs, Mr McNabb remained unmoved, his arms folded across his chest. Felicity tried to imagine him firing the shot that left Mr Reeves dead on the village green, but she couldn't picture it. Mr McNabb seemed somehow neater and more careful than that. She considered the route she would need to take through the packed church in order to reach him. It would be easy for him to slip out of the door. She'd have to move quickly.

A hymn was sung before the closing of the service, which lasted not more than half an hour in total. Felicity's write-up of the event wouldn't make thrilling reading, but sensationalism wasn't ever the goal of the parish newsletter.

Father Neil looked at his lectern for a moment, then back at the congregation. "For anyone wishing it, a memorial reception is being held at our village's inn. Our thanks to Mr Chesterton, landlord of the Cat and Cream, for offering this facility to our village in its hour of need."

Had Mr Chesterton been present at the memorial service, he would have sprung to his feet to absorb any praise or gratitude directed his way, but he must have been busy at the inn with preparations for the reception, which was no doubt financially more worthwhile than his presence at the memorial, for no such acknowledgment came.

With the ceremony closed, Felicity jumped out of her seat, intent on making a beeline for Mr McNabb, but she and her grandmother quickly became boxed in by people making their way to the doors, and Felicity lost sight of Mr McNabb in the crowd. She admonished herself for not having been more strategic in her choice of pew.

"Father Neil does a lovely service, doesn't he?" said Mrs Winterpole, who, like Felicity and her grandmother, shuffled forward to join the slow-moving throng of people heading towards the church doors.

"He certainly does," replied Lady Henrietta. "I only hope he's able to provide any mourners attending my memorial such inspiration and comfort."

"I've already written some notes on what I'd like said at my service," said Mrs Winterpole.

Lady Henrietta nodded knowingly. "I've done the same. One can't rely on one's relatives to give these matters the right amount of attention. Young people are so busy with their own issues these days."

Moving at a snail's pace along the church's busy central aisle, Felicity did her best not to listen to Lady Henrietta and Mrs Winterpole's rather morbid discussion as she hopelessly scanned the crowd for a sign of Mr McNabb. Alex also seemed to have disappeared, while Lord Northcote's gamekeepers had moved to the front of the church where Mr Reeves' maid still sat sobbing. The older of the two workers had positioned himself beside Nora on the pew, his cap in his hands and his head bowed. He seemed to be doing his best to comfort the girl while the younger gamekeeper stood awkwardly a short distance away, a sour look on his face. Felicity wondered what the relationship between Nora and the gamekeepers might be.

"Are you looking for someone, Felicity dear?" asked Lady Henrietta, turning to her granddaughter.

Felicity frowned. "There was someone I was hoping to speak to, but he's gone."

"Was it me you wanted to talk to, Lady Felicity?"

Father Neil had approached from the pews on the other side of the aisle, his wiry frame towering over her.

"Hello, Father Neil," said Felicity. "Actually, no. I was looking to speak to someone else."

"That's a pity," said the vicar with a remonstrative lift of his eyebrows, "because I would certainly like to have a word with you."

Chapter Thirteen

As All Angels church continued to empty of parishioners, Felicity squirmed under the vicar's gaze. He could be quite imposing when he wanted to be.

"Do you need to speak to me this very moment, Father Neil?" asked Felicity.

"Yes, my lady," he said. His usually gentle gaze was hard. "In private."

"Of course," replied Felicity. Was the vicar angry? She'd never known him to be. Perhaps he had something to tell her about the murder to include in the newsletter. "If that's all right with Grandmama?" Felicity turned to Lady Henrietta, but the dowager was deep in conversation with the Broughtons, discussing the placement of alpine plants in their new rockery.

Felicity followed Father Neil through the transept and into the spacious hall that had been added to the church before the war. It was where the village's Sunday school lessons were held, and chairs for this purpose were stacked against the walls. The rain had cleared, and the sun shone through high windows onto the hall's red carpet.

The vicar put his hands behind his back. "Allow me to be frank, Lady Felicity," his voice echoing in the space.

"I wouldn't want you to be anything else, Father Neil."

"I received your message via my housekeeper yesterday evening. I understand you're planning a special edition of the parish newsletter dedicated to poor Mr Reeves and the awful business surrounding his demise on our village green."

"That's correct," said Felicity. "It's our duty to keep the parishioners informed."

The vicar took a deep breath. "As you know, my lady, I've given you a lot of room when it comes to the newsletter. You do a wonderful job as editor, and readership has never been better."

Felicity glowed inwardly. "Thank you for saying so, Father Neil."

The vicar furrowed his brow. "However, while I don't like to be tyrannical in such matters, this special edition is something I simply cannot allow."

Felicity grimaced. The vicar's disapproval was a blow she hadn't expected. "Why ever not?"

"I cannot allow you to write about Mr Reeves' death in our parish newsletter."

"But..." began Felicity, confused. "But how could we possibly not write about it? Wouldn't it be rather odd not to mention it?"

The vicar shifted uneasily. A draft of air moved the wisps of grey hair that haloed his head. "Mr Reeves' death will be mentioned as a memorial announcement in the next regular edition, but there will be no special edition and no special reports on the murder or its investigation."

Felicity's mouth fell open. She snapped it shut. "But I already booked a print run. Mr Duggan's expecting my copy by midday."

"I'm aware of that, my lady, because Mr Duggan telephoned the rectory earlier this morning. He wanted to confirm the delivery time, but I told him the special edition has been cancelled."

Felicity shook her head. Without the parish newsletter, how would she respond to the murder, counter any rumours about Lord Northcote, and prove her brother and Alex wrong about her abilities as a journalist?

"Father Neil, don't you think this is rather unfair? Forgive me for pointing out the obvious, but I am the newsletter's editor, and the issue I was preparing is practically finished."

The vicar sighed. "I'm extremely grateful for your talents and dedication. The whole parish is. But you must remember, my lady, that while you are the editor, the newsletter is paid for with church funds, and it can only be published with my approval. And I do not approve of this."

Donations from the Quick family accounted for a large proportion of the parish's finances, but Felicity wouldn't stoop to mentioning that. "Can you explain to me why you don't approve?" she said. "Perhaps there's been some kind of misunderstanding."

"It's simply not appropriate, my lady."

"But why?"

"You seem to forget that it's a parish newsletter, not a newspaper. We don't have a duty to report on events as they happen. The purpose of the newsletter is to serve the parish."

"But sharing news and explaining local events is serving the parish, isn't it?"

Father Neil let out a sigh of exasperation. "Lady Felicity, this tragic death at the heart of our community has created an enormous amount of work for the church. Let's meet next week and talk about a new edition of the newsletter. I'll read through what you've already written, and we can decide together what to include. I think that will be the best way forward. Wouldn't you agree?"

Felicity paused. She didn't agree. In fact, the whole matter gave her rather an uneasy feeling. Father Neil never usually wanted to inspect her copy.

Clearing her throat, she said, "Is there something you don't want the parishioners to know, Father Neil?"

Clouds chased across the sun, making the Sunday school room suddenly dark.

"What are you trying to say, Lady Felicity? Do you think I have something to hide?" The vicar's solemn face softened with amusement. "Goodness. This nasty business certainly has everyone riled up, but I never imagined you of all people would be susceptible to such wild ideas."

Felicity narrowed her eyes at the vicar as anger bubbled up in her chest. She was so exceedingly tired of being obstructed at every turn. That was why, when she opened her mouth and said what she did, there was nothing she could do to stop herself.

Felicity strode along the now-empty gravel path of All Angels' church as it began raining again. She tugged up the collar of her coat to cover the back of her neck, but the umbrella Felicity and her grandmother had brought with them was gone from the church's vestibule. Lady Henrietta must have taken it with her, presumably to the Cat and Cream for the reception, which meant Felicity was going to get rather wet on her walk back to Bradley Court.

She couldn't attend the memorial reception. She'd just been undermined and humiliated. Again. It was the second time in two days. First, Jasper had turned Felicity into a trainee and given her dream assignment to someone else. Then, the vicar had cancelled her special edition of the parish newsletter, even though she'd already been telling the villagers about it.

To top it all off, with an impulsiveness Felicity had never known, she'd told the vicar she was quitting the parish newsletter and marched out of the Sunday school hall. Despite her plans to hand in her notice the day before, Felicity already felt pangs of regret, especially with her career in newspaper journalism going precisely nowhere. However, awareness of her bleak prospects hadn't prevented her from doing it. The act of quitting had given her a sense of power, of truly being in control. Yet the feeling had been fleeting.

Turning up the village high street towards the lane back to Bradley Court and away from the Cat and Cream, Felicity battled a sense of gloomy discouragement as the wind drove the rain directly into her face. What would she do now?

"Lady Felicity!" A voice rose above the wind. "Yoo-hoo! Lady Felicity!"

Felicity turned, the rain lashing the back of her rubberised coat. Mrs Fry stepped out of the bakery. Balanced deftly in one hand, she carried an enormous tray wrapped in tinfoil. With the other hand, she gestured to Felicity.

"Oh, Mrs Fry." Felicity approached the baker's wife obediently, but she didn't want to be chastised about her decision not to join the reception at the inn and considered telling a harmless lie about having a headache.

"I saw him again, you know," said Mrs Fry, before Felicity could proffer her excuses.

Felicity pulled her toque down to shield her eyes from the rain. "Saw who?"

"The memorial reception is much busier than Mr Chesterton thought it would be, so he asked me if I could bring down some more slices, which of course I'm happy to do. Me and Mr Fry always like to bake extra, because you never know. I was on my way out of the inn, and who should I see but that gentleman again. The one I told you was asking after poor Mr Reeves. The Scottish gentleman with the fancy moustache."

Felicity no longer had an article to write, but that didn't mean she'd lost all sense of curiosity about Mr Reeves' demise.

"Will you be joining us at the reception, my lady?"

"Actually," said Felicity, any imaginings of a headache having vanished. "I think I shall."

Chapter Fourteen

The Cat and Cream's dining room was in the simple style typical of the Devonshire countryside, with white-washed walls and black wooden beams across its low ceiling. The seats at the small, round tables were full with memorial service attendees who were solemnly enjoying steaming cups of tea with milk and coffee served with cream, all while speaking to each other in appropriately sombre tones. There was also a buffet table covered in an appropriately limited but no less delicious-looking selection of cakes and slices, which Mrs Fry was topping up.

Felicity's grandmother was at a table in the far corner, engaged in deep conversation with Mrs Winterpole and a few other ladies from the Lower Diddleton Plant and Floral Society, but Mr McNabb was nowhere to be seen. The inn's landlord, Mr Chesterton, was, however, present, his wiry frame bent over a malfunctioning coffee urn on the far side of the room. Felicity no longer needed his input for the newsletter, but he could still be useful, so she crossed the dining room.

"Mr Chesterton, I'd like to have a word," she said in a tone that indicated she was in no mood to be brushed off.

The landlord straightened himself. "Ah, Lady Felicity. How good of you to join us. I'm aware I still owe you some of my time, but as

I'm sure you can appreciate, there's not much I can spare you on a busy day such as this. And, of course, there's the inquest tomorrow to prepare for. It's being held here, you know." Mr Chesterton raised his eyebrows smugly. "At the Cat and Cream."

With Felicity's plans for the parish newsletter now cancelled, Mr Chesterton's lack of availability for an interview was of no consequence. "Actually," she said, "it was a guest of yours with whom I was hoping to speak. An older gentleman with a grey moustache waxed into curls. Where might I find him?"

The landlord folded his arms over his chest. "Lady Felicity, I am the owner of a village inn, not a gaoler. As long as my guests pay the correct rate for their rooms, they are free to come and go as they please. I don't keep tabs on them."

"But I'm told he was here just now. You surely must have seen him."

With a queue now growing for the coffee urn, Mr Chesterton spoke curtly and in low tones. "As a matter of fact, my lady, I didn't. But even if I had, and with all the respect I have for you and your family, I wouldn't divulge his or any other guest's activities or whereabouts to you or any other member of the general public. If the police asked, that would be a different matter, of course, but as I've already explained, I offer my guests hospitality. I do not chaperone them. If you want to speak to one of my guests, I suggest you leave a message at reception. That's the proper way to go about it."

Felicity lifted an eyebrow. "What an excellent idea," she said, aware that she'd met another dead end with the landlord. "Thank you, Mr Chesterton."

Leaving the innkeeper with his broken coffee urn, Felicity attempted to orient herself in the direction of the inn's reception desk, already pondering what kind of message she would leave for Mr McNabb. Should she arrange a meeting with him? If so, where? It would be unconnected to any publication, but Felicity refused to be shut out of the biggest story ever to happen in Lower Diddleton. She had to be involved.

Felicity was about to follow a sign that read *Reception* down a narrow floral-papered corridor off the dining room when she spotted Nora Andrews, Mr Reeves' maid, standing alone beside the buffet table, her rather puffy eyes scanning the full dining room as though unsure of where to sit. With her narrow shoulders, thin nose, and watery brown eyes, she seemed a frail, timid creature, and Felicity felt pity for the girl. Pity and a potent dose of curiosity.

"Miss Andrews?" said Felicity, offering Nora a kindly smile.

The girl nodded hesitatingly. Even with her features red from crying, she had a pretty, delicate face. In her hand was a plate with an untouched cherry slice.

"I don't believe we've yet met. I'm Lady Felicity Quick, of Bradley Court. You worked for Mr Reeves, did you not? May I say how terribly sorry I am for the loss of your employer. I can only imagine how awful this past day or so must have been for you."

Nora nodded some more and sniffed. Her eyes shone, threatening more tears, and her pupils darted back and forth, unable to hold Felicity's gaze. "Thank you, my lady," she said in a voice barely above a whisper.

"I'm sorry to say I didn't know Mr Reeves very well," continued Felicity, resisting the temptation to pull out her notebook. "What was he like?"

Nora's eyes snapped to Felicity's. "He was always good to me, my lady," she said, a tear escaping from the corner of her eye. "He was always very good to me." Her accent indicated she was from Devon or one of the neighbouring counties.

Felicity's heart hurt a little for the young girl, who couldn't have been much older than eighteen and was clearly extremely upset. Felicity remembered her promise to herself when she was considering interviewing Nora for the newsletter: she didn't want to intrude on anyone's grief, so she put her curiosity about Mr Reeves to one side.

"Do you have any family or friends nearby?" Felicity asked gently. "Anyone that can help you?"

Nora nodded. "Yes, I..." Her voice trailed off as her mournful eyes settled on the floral corridor leading to the Cat and Cream's reception desk. There, framed in the opening at the other end of the passageway, was Mr McNabb, his high-collared coat and old-fashioned moustache unmistakable.

Nora quickly put down her plate with its uneaten slice. "I'm sorry. I have to go," she said and scampered towards the door leading onto the inn's rain-soaked courtyard.

Felicity shook her head, a little discombobulated. Had the sight of Mr McNabb frightened Nora, or had Felicity said something to upset the dead man's maid? She would ponder the matter later. It was time to speak to the mysterious Mr McNabb.

With a small leather valise on the floor by his feet, Mr McNabb stood waiting for the young clerk behind the inn's reception desk to finish a task. When Felicity arrived beside him, Mr McNabb turned to her, acknowledging her presence with a polite smile, before looking away. Two uniformed police officers — presumably from Exeter as Felicity didn't recognise them — stood talking to one another next to the stairs leading up to the guest rooms. Their proximity both reassured and emboldened her. Even if Mr McNabb had something to do with Mr Reeves' murder, he surely wouldn't try anything at the inn.

"Excuse me," said Felicity. "Mr McNabb?"

The man with the moustache turned back to her, his brow creasing with surprise. "Yes?"

"I'm terribly sorry to trouble you," continued Felicity. "I realise we're not yet acquainted, but I heard you knew Mr Reeves, the man whose body was found on our village green just yesterday. Is that correct?"

Mr McNabb's curled, grey moustache quivered. "And who, may I ask, might you be?" He indeed had a rich Scottish accent. "Are you a journalist? Because if you are, I'm not interested in talking to the press."

"I'm Lady Felicity Quick," she said. "And I'm not speaking to you as a journalist," she added in all honesty.

Mr McNabb lowered his eyebrows. "And what might your interest be in Mr Reeves, my lady?"

Felicity thought for a moment. "I've lived in the area all my life, and nothing of this sort has ever taken place here before. I want to know how something so terrible ever came to happen in our quiet village."

"You're simply curious? Nothing more?"

"Yes," said Felicity forthrightly. "There's no law against wanting to understand a matter, is there?"

Mr McNabb eyed Felicity with a mixture of impatience and suspicion. "My dear, as I'm sure you're aware, the matter of Mr Reeves' passing has the full attention of our friends in the Devon County Constabulary." He gestured towards the uniformed officers, who were now in discussion with a Homburg-hatted detective. "You can rest assured that considering what has happened, anything I might know about Mr Reeves has been shared with officers of the law."

"I heard you were investigating him yourself," said Felicity. "Even before the man was killed. Is that not so?"

Mr McNabb narrowed his eyes. "While I understand your curiosity about Mr Reeves' passing, my lady, I would recommend leaving the matter to the police."

The clerk approached the counter, holding out an envelope and a folded piece of paper. "Your invoice is in the envelope, Mr McNabb, and here's the message that was left at the reception for you earlier. As per your request, there should be a taxi waiting outside to take you to Sweetbrooke station."

Thanking the clerk, Mr McNabb unfolded the paper and read the message. As he did so, his face tightened. "Who left this note for me?" he asked the clerk.

"I couldn't say, sir. We found it left here on the reception desk early this morning."

Mr McNabb refolded the note. "Change of plan," he said. "I shan't be needing the taxi. Can I book in for another night?"

The clerk blew out a breath as he opened the large leather-bound registration book. "We might not have the same room available, sir, as we're rather busy at the moment, but I'll do my best for you. Would you like to take a seat in the bar while I make arrangements? I'll send word through to you as soon as I've found a room."

"I'll do just that," said Mr McNabb. He turned to Felicity. "It was a pleasure to meet you, my lady." He lifted his valise and stepped away from the reception desk, making his way towards the door leading to the Cat and Cream's bar.

"Lady Felicity," said the reception clerk, looking up from the registration book. "So sorry to have kept you waiting. What can I do for you?"

"Oh," said Felicity, retreating from the counter with a polite shake of her head, unsure whether to follow Mr McNabb. "Nothing. Thank you."

She'd hit another obstacle, only this time it felt inevitable rather than frustrating. Of course, Felicity was curious about the murder. Everyone was. So why should she have the right to know more about it than anyone else? Mr McNabb was under no obligation to speak to her.

A second detective joined the discussion by the stairs leading up to the guest rooms. Felicity thought again about the N she'd seen in the mud next to the dead man's hand. Maybe the police from Exeter, who doubtlessly had more experience with murder enquiries than Sergeant Hodgkins and Constable Price, would know better what to do with the information than the local officers. Indeed, she could tell the police from Exeter about what she'd seen, then forget about the matter entirely. She no longer had an article to write, and if Lord Northcote was innocent, which Felicity was certain he was, then he shouldn't need her help in proving it. Felicity would find something else to concentrate on, be that society reporting or helping her grandmother care for her prize-winning roses. She would continue as if there'd never been a murder in Lower Diddleton. Her life would return to being quiet and peaceful, just as the village would eventually also do.

Felicity again approached the reception desk. "Actually, there is something you might help me with," she said, addressing the clerk. "Where might I find the detectives leading the Reeves investigation?"

The clerk pointed to a doorway to one side of the reception. "Down that corridor is where the Exeter police have established their headquarters, my lady. I believe you'll find the gentleman you're looking for down there."

Felicity made her way along the narrow corridor, this one decorated with hunt-themed wallpaper featuring the motif of a duck being chased from a patch of reeds by a dog. As she approached the end of the corridor, it was possible to hear the discussion taking place in the room beyond.

"There's nothing else for it. It's going to mean another trip to Sittingdon Hall."

Felicity stopped and listened.

"Lord Northcote won't like it."

"Like or dislike's got nothing to do with it. We're here to do our work. The gun we've found is his, and there are questions that need to be asked. And answered."

Felicity's blood ran cold. Were the police closing in on Lord Northcote?

A uniformed officer coming in the opposite direction, his helmet under his arm, did his best to pass Felicity without knocking into her, which was difficult given the narrowness of the space.

"Sorry, miss," he said as he passed.

"That's quite all right," replied Felicity with automatic politeness, but really, there was nothing at all right about the situation.

Uncle Basil was close to being arrested for murder.

Slowly, Felicity withdrew from the corridor. She knew it was wrong, but she couldn't tell the Exeter detectives about the N in the mud, not now, for it would surely seal Lord Northcote's fate. What could she do to help? She needed time to think. A walk would help her come to her senses.

Felicity crossed the inn's reception, nodding politely to the clerk as she went, but before reaching the door leading onto the village high street, something on the floor caught her eye. It was a folded piece of paper. She stooped, picked it up, and with a glance to check no one was watching her, she unfolded it.

Letters had been cut from newspaper and carefully pasted into place to form a message:

Tonight, 11 o'clock, in the churchyard. I'll tell you everything.

Felicity looked around again. The police and hotel staff were all busy, so no one had seen her pick up the note. It had to be the message that had been left at reception for Mr McNabb. The paper hadn't been on the floor when Felicity first arrived at the inn's reception.

"Felicity, dear. There you are, at last. I've been looking for you."

Felicity tucked the note into the pocket of her dress as her grandmother bustled along the narrow corridor from the dining room. Arriving at the inn's reception, Lady Henrietta cut an imposing figure in black fur and lace, her hands resting on the silver handle of her umbrella.

But it wasn't the sight of Lady Henrietta that made Felicity's heart sink.

Behind her grandmother, squeezing along the narrow corridor, was Jasper.

"Hello, Felicity," he said, standing before her in a dark grey suit and royal blue tie. "I think you and I better have a little talk, don't you?"

Chapter Fifteen

Upon returning to Lower Diddleton from Bristol, Jasper had gone to All Angels church hoping to catch some of the memorial service. The service having been rather brief, he'd arrived after its end, but Jasper's visit to the church hadn't been in vain. Father Neil took the opportunity to inform him of what Felicity had been planning for the parish newsletter and what the vicar referred to as Felicity's 'worrisome' interest in the murder.

"You know I don't like to impose rules, Felicity," Jasper told her in the inn's reception within earshot of the clerk and nearby police officers. "But I simply cannot sit back and watch you get mixed up in this awful business."

In Jasper's claret-coloured Bentley, which Jasper himself drove back to Bradley Court, he'd told Felicity they'd discuss her future as a journalist after the furore around the murder had settled down. "Very well," Felicity had said coolly, but it was precisely the furore around the murder that she didn't want to let pass her by. How could she not be involved when a close family friend was now the prime suspect? It didn't help that Alex was likely at that very moment in his room at the Cat and Cream, typing up the story that would appear on tomorrow's front page, probably pointing to Lord Northcote as the guilty party.

However, once back at Bradley Court, short of storming off to her bedroom like a petulant child, there was nothing Felicity could do except accompany her brother and grandmother into Bradley Court's dining room for a distinctly awkward family lunch.

"Cook has made pea and asparagus salad," said Lady Henrietta with unusual brightness as she handed her umbrella to a footman. "You enjoy a salad, don't you, Felicity dear?"

Jasper sat at one end of the long, highly polished table, Lady Henrietta sat at the other, and Felicity sat between them, with Pip curled on the red velvet cushion of the chair next to her. She pushed her peas around with her fork, finding it difficult to take part in the stilted lunchtime conversation. Jasper had decreed that there was to be no more discussion of Mr Reeves' murder for the rest of the day, but it was a rather difficult topic to manoeuvre around.

As the footman topped up their water glasses, Jasper tried to explain the challenges of managing the demands of the Western Daily News' advertisers, but he was put off when Lady Henrietta failed in adequately concealing a yawn. The subject was then changed to the concerns of Lower Diddleton's Plant and Floral Society about the possible cancellation of the village's summer fete. As Lady Henrietta attempted to explain the matter without mentioning the murder as the reason for the cancellation, Felicity experienced a certain amount of inward glee at watching Jasper squirm, a grimace under his moustache as their grandmother circled ever closer to the forbidden topic.

"It would be an entire year's work wasted," said Lady Henrietta. "All those flowers and vegetables are grown purely for the fete. I don't suppose either of you know anything about the care and time that go into growing a prize-winning vegetable marrow or a first-class salvia. And Lady Northcote is, of course, tremendously upset about the police trampling all over her gardens. That won't help her fuchsias one bit, as they can be awfully temperamental."

Felicity looked up from her peas. "Have the police been searching Sittingdon Hall?"

"Yes, dear. They—"

Jasper cut Lady Henrietta off with a sharp cough, followed by a glare of warning. She looked from Felicity to Jasper, clearly dismayed at having been interrupted.

"Well," continued the dowager. "I mean, there are things I suppose I ought not say."

Felicity blinked innocently. "May I not even be kept updated about what's happening to Uncle Basil and Aunt Penelope?"

Jasper drummed his fingers on the dining room table. "My obligations to the newspaper may mean I don't see the Northcotes as often as I ought to, but they're both safe and well, Felicity. You can be reassured of that."

"Safe and well," said Felicity slowly, "but being investigated by the police?"

Pip's ears twitched, indicating he was only pretending to be asleep.

Jasper let out a sigh. "Really. I thought we agreed to leave the topic alone."

"But Lord and Lady Northcote are practically family," pressed Felicity. "Don't I have a right to know if they're in trouble with the police?"

Looking to Lady Henrietta for support but receiving only a shrug in response, Jasper turned reluctantly to Felicity. "The police have found a double-barrelled rifle, which they believe to be the murder weapon."

"And it belongs to Uncle Basil?" said Felicity, her mouth going dry as she remembered what she'd overheard the detectives saying at the Cat and Cream.

"Unfortunately, yes," confirmed Jasper. "It does."

Lady Henrietta put down her knife and fork and addressed Felicity. "We should trust in the police to do their work, dear."

Felicity looked from her brother to her grandmother. "But do you think Uncle Basil did it?"

"It doesn't matter who we think did it," said Jasper, his face betraying his dismay at the situation. "What matters is that the police find who committed the crime so that person, whoever he may be, can face justice."

"It wasn't Lord Northcote though, was it?" said Felicity. She looked at her grandmother. "Was it?"

"I must support your brother in this, my dear," said Lady Henrietta with a frown. "Let's leave such matters to the police to worry about."

"But Grandmama," Felicity said imploringly, unable to understand her family's reticence on the matter. "Do you really think Uncle Basil capable of murder?"

Lady Henrietta fixed Felicity with her lavender-blue gaze. "No, Felicity, I do not believe Lord Northcote to be capable of murder."

A modicum of relief lightened Felicity's heart.

"But then again," added her grandmother, "I'm not an expert in these matters. The police are."

Felicity frowned. "What if the police get it wrong? Miscarriages of justice do happen."

"Now, now, Cici," said Jasper. "This is exactly why I didn't want us talking anymore about the murder today. Let's not go getting upset about things."

"My dear, one can't think like that," said Lady Henrietta. "One can't question everything all the time. In doing so, one would simply go mad. One has to have faith that justice will prevail. Isn't that right, Jasper?"

"Yes," he said stiffly. "That's right, Grandmama. Now, can we continue our meal without another word about this bally awful murder?"

Felicity remained unsatisfied with her family's responses, but out of respect for her brother and grandmother, she went back to pushing around her peas. After further awkward conversation about summer pruning and the opening of a new golf course near Exmouth, Felicity turned down dessert and took Pip up to her room. As the Yorkie curled onto the ottoman at the end of her bed, Felicity flopped down onto her mattress, eyeing the thick stack of typed paper piled on her desk, which she'd intended to hand to the printer that very day.

In a way, perhaps Jasper was right to insist on avoidance of the topic of Mr Reeves' murder. Maybe he'd been right to warn her away from the whole affair from the very beginning. What if Lord Northcote was proven to be the killer, after all? Felicity would have made a fool of herself trying to defend him in the parish newsletter, which the vicar thankfully stopped her from publishing.

As she stretched listlessly across her bed, her notepad poked awkwardly into her thigh. She reached into the pocket of her dress and pulled out the pad and pencil. With it came the note she'd found on the floor at the Cat and Cream, which must have been dropped by Mr McNabb. She picked it up off her bed and unfolded it once again.

Tonight, 11 o'clock, in the churchyard. I'll tell you everything.

Felicity had yet to consider what to do with the note, but one thing was certain. The idea of being told everything was extremely appealing.

Chapter Sixteen

Following an afternoon of distracted reading in her room — a detective novel in which Felicity felt the guilty party had been made too obvious rather early in the book — there was an awkward family dinner that was kept rather brief thanks to Jasper's work commitments. After dinner, Felicity played several hands of piquet with Lady Henrietta before returning to her room, where she again attempted to read as she waited. At long last, the grandfather clock in the entrance hall struck a quarter past ten, and Felicity crept down the carpeted stairs to Bradley Court's entrance hall.

No one noticed her movements besides Pip, who was keen on his rest and had no objection to being left in bed at such an hour. The entire house was asleep except for Jasper, who was busy with newspaper business in his study at the other end of the house, and a few members of household staff. The staff moved like clockwork around the house, closing curtains and returning cushions to their rightful places, which allowed Felicity to set a path on which she could reliably avoid them.

Bradley Court's solid oak front doors were so well maintained they were noiseless upon opening and closing. After passing through the formal gardens, which Felicity knew well enough to navigate with her eyes closed, she came to the end of an avenue lined with beech trees where she needed to climb over a gate. She did this with ease, having changed into a set of old tweeds — her notebook and pencil tucked into the pocket of the skirt — and a sturdy pair of Oxfords she used when walking on the moors.

Leaving the cover of the trees behind, Felicity stepped onto the lane leading down into Lower Diddleton. A full moon hung like a clean, white dinner plate high in the sky, lighting the hedgerows and fields with an ethereal silver. The occasional cloud covered the moon and cast the lane into deep shadow, but the darkness never lasted long. The night was as peaceful as it was beautiful.

Yet despite the night's charms, Felicity knew that Jasper and even her grandmother would be most displeased by her actions, which was why she was performing them in secret. She'd told no one where she was going, but it didn't matter, because she wouldn't do anything silly. She was going to listen. That was all.

It was surreal to arrive in Lower Diddleton to find the shop fronts dark and the streets empty of people. There were lights on at the Cat and Cream, where some guests were seemingly still awake. Crossing the village green, Felicity stuck to the shadows of the trees and hurried between the police vehicles still parked on the grass. She was especially careful to ensure that a small group of uniformed police officers didn't notice her pass, as they stood by the pond smoking cigarettes and talking in hushed voices. Her tweed jacket and skirt, deliberately chosen for their murky brown tones, no doubt helped her remain camouflaged.

The clock in the church's bell tower struck half past ten by the time Felicity reached the lychgate. She avoided the gravel pathway, which would crunch underfoot, choosing instead to tread through the grass between the gravestones, scanning her surroundings all the while to make sure she was alone in the churchyard. With no one to notice her movements, Felicity took up a crouching position behind a large yew tree, which cast a deep shadow against the wall of All Angels church, and there she waited.

The plan was simple: Felicity would listen to whatever Mr McNabb's informant told him, taking notes as she saw fit. She would then use what she learned to decide her next steps. She hoped that whatever she heard would put her mind at rest about Lord Northcote's involvement in the case and help her finally decide about what to do with the N she'd seen written in the mud.

It didn't take long before Mr McNabb arrived, his footsteps on the gravel path announcing him. He was calm as he waited in the churchyard and smoked a pipe, the clouds of smoke rising and dissipating into the night. He examined the text on a few of the headstones as he waited, some of which had posies of fresh flowers on them.

Felicity shifted a little as her lower legs became numb from crouching. She dared not move too much for fear of making a sound and alerting Mr McNabb to her presence, but she froze when another set of footsteps came crunching up the churchyard path. From behind the old yew, Felicity could see only the newcomer's feet, which were clad in a pair of heavy boots. It had to be the informant who'd left the note for Mr McNabb at the inn. Trying not to move too much, Felicity craned her neck to try to see who it was.

"So. You're here to tell me everything, are you?" Mr McNabb spoke first, his Scottish burr unmistakable, though he'd moved to a position on the churchyard path where only his shoes were visible from Felicity's hiding place behind the old yew. "Perhaps you can start by telling me who you are." Mr McNabb's tone suggested he was speaking to someone younger than himself or of a lower social class. He certainly wouldn't address someone like Lord Northcote in such an informal manner.

A cloud slipped across the moon, plunging the churchyard into darkness. What little Felicity could see of the situation became nothing at all. There was a loud bang. Then another. The brief flashes from the weapon's muzzle lit up the night beyond the tree branches.

An understanding of what she was witnessing didn't come to Felicity immediately, but when a man's voice cried out in pain, she realised what had happened and was about to scream in fright when a hand clamped over her mouth from behind, and she was silenced.

Chapter Seventeen

"Try to stay calm. Don't make a sound." The man whose hand covered Felicity's mouth was close enough for her to feel his breath on her cheek as he whispered his instructions. "Nod if you've understood."

After a brief hesitation, Felicity nodded. What choice did she have?

The hand released from her mouth, and Felicity turned. Crouched beside her was Alex, a finger to his lips, his broad shoulders hunched in the yew's shadow. How had he got so close without her noticing? Still, it was a relief to see someone she knew, even if he was a rival.

Footsteps, now running, crunched hard along the churchyard path. The clouds shifted, and the moonlight returned, casting everything in an eerie shade of silver. Through the branches of the yew, there was no trace visible of Mr McNabb.

"Has Mr McNabb been shot?" hissed Felicity, her heart pounding harder than it perhaps ever had. "Oh, heavens. Has there been another murder?"

"Possibly," said Alex, looking calmly over his shoulder towards the village high street. "But I'd say we have a rather pressing decision to make."

There were several sharp bursts on a policeman's whistle as boots pounded the high street pavement.

"We have a choice," said Alex. "Either we stay here to be discovered by the police, or we run."

"But Mr McNabb..." Felicity peered between the yew branches. "He might be hurt. He could be dying. Shouldn't we do something?"

"The police will arrive any moment." Alex spoke quickly yet calmly. "Or do you want to explain yourself to Jasper when the police bring you home?"

Alex had an extremely good point, but why was he so keen to help Felicity avoid her brother's disapproval? There wasn't time for questions. The policemen's shouts were drawing nearer.

Felicity looked at Alex. "Let's go."

Alex gave a firm nod of acknowledgment. "Stay close."

Crouched low, Alex led the way, sticking to the wall of the church until they reached the thin strip of grassy ground next to a high, granite wall bordering the neighbouring property.

Alex crossed the open ground quickly and got on one knee beside the wall. Offering his knitted fingers to Felicity, he whispered, "Climb over. As fast as you can. I'll give you a lift."

Felicity frowned. The property next door was a yard where one of the local farming families kept horse carts in which they gave rides to tourists. It would be perfectly possible to hide among the carts and not be seen from the village high street, which must by now have been filling with police and bystanders, but Felicity still hesitated. She'd never climbed such a high wall before.

"Here!" The police were in the churchyard on the other side of the church, where Felicity and Alex had been just moments before. "Got a man down. He's in a bad way." They must have found Mr McNabb. "Hopkins, get back to the inn and ring for an ambulance. Whoever did this can't have got far, lads. Let's find him. Where's Countess?"

"It's now or never, Felicity." Alex turned his face away from his hands. "You've nothing to worry about. I shan't look."

It certainly wasn't prudishness holding Felicity back, but the idea of being brought back to Bradley Court in a police motor spurred her on. She hurried across the grass and placed an Oxford on Alex's hands, grabbed the top of the wall, and hauled herself upwards, Alex pushing her from below.

It was surprisingly easy to reach the top, but being rather inexperienced in the scaling of walls, Felicity had given no consideration to her landing on the other side. Sadly, it was too late to turn it into anything elegant. Her skirt tangled between her knees, and she dropped like a baby squirrel falling out of a tree, narrowly missing a stack of cartwheels as her limbs scrambled in the air. Bruised though she certainly would be, Felicity's landing on the slightly muddy ground thankfully made very little noise. Alex landed beside her, as agile as a cat, and together they ran for cover behind a cart that had a sheet of waxed canvas pulled protectively over its seats.

A dog could be heard barking in the churchyard.

"Countess has the scent, sir," called one of the policemen. "The fellow must have gone over the wall at the back of the graveyard and into that field."

"Good work, Brown. Hunt him down, lads. We're not letting him get away this time."

Felicity sighed with relief. The search for the shooter was going in the opposite direction, where the fields of Lord Northcote's lands met the church's boundary wall. Although that didn't bode well for Uncle Basil, she couldn't help but be thankful that the chances of Jasper finding out about her escapade in the churchyard were dwindling.

"They're going the other way," whispered Felicity.

"Good, but we can't stay here. They'll search the place soon enough." Alex gestured for Felicity to follow him. "Let's keep moving."

Stooped low, they moved swiftly from cart to cart, stopping to check for policemen and curious locals who might spot them from the high street, as the gates to the cart yard were never closed. Alex moved with precision and efficiency. Felicity wondered if his skilfulness in concealment and escape had been learned during the war. She did her best to copy him, moving quietly from one hiding place to another.

Next to the cart yard was a row of small terraced cottages separated from the high street by a hedge of neatly clipped beech. The hedge cast a long, dense shadow onto the pavement. Alex slipped into the inky black.

"Felicity," came Alex's disembodied voice from within the darkness of the shadows. "We need to keep going."

She hesitated. She barely knew Alex. Could she trust him? Did she have the choice of whether to do so? Of all the options open to her, following Alex seemed the most sensible. He was rather competent at evading the police, and Felicity couldn't imagine Jasper would place so much faith in a man who wasn't at least trustworthy. Her brother's original plan was for Felicity to train with Alex.

As she slipped into the shadows behind him, she felt a rush of fear and excitement, similar to what one experiences on a ride at the fair.

Chapter Eighteen

Reappearing from the shadows, his blond hair pale in the moonlight, Alex took the turning at the end of the terraced cottages. Felicity was slightly breathless as she caught up with him, his stride being longer than hers. She saw now that Alex was in a waistcoat and shirtsleeves and had the cuffs of his shirt turned up on his forearms. Felicity was glad she'd chosen to wear sensible walking shoes, as the police would likely have caught her by now had she not.

Without speaking, she and Alex walked briskly along a furrowed trackway that led away from Lower Diddleton and towards the hamlet of Oakridge Head. The shouts of policemen and motors starting up could be heard from the village, but Felicity's heart rate was growing calmer, despite having to walk faster than normal to keep up with Alex. As they moved further away from the village, the view became one of rolling fields bathed in silver light, dotted with groups of trees and edged with dark hedges. The occasional shadow of a cloud scudded across the open ground.

"For someone fresh from London," Felicity said, still a little breathless, "you know Lower Diddleton and its surroundings awfully well."

Alex broke from scanning the fields and hedgerows on either side of the trackway to glance at Felicity. "I've walked around the place once or twice since arriving."

They passed an orchard full of gnarled apple trees, their silhouettes almost lifelike. Anyone could have been hiding in the shadows, including the man with the gun from the churchyard.

Felicity swallowed. "Are we safe?"

Alex flashed another glance at her, his blue eyes pale in the moonlight. "Nowhere in the world is one-hundred percent safe."

She frowned. "How tremendously reassuring."

"But to my estimation," continued Alex unruffled, "if the shooter in the churchyard wanted us dead, he'd have shot us by now."

Felicity's heart gave a little bounce. "Again, that's incredibly comforting. Where are we going?"

"I'm bringing you home. To Bradley Court."

Felicity raised her eyebrows. "Via Oakridge Head? You certainly do know your way around."

Alex said nothing in reply. The only sounds were their footsteps on the rough surface of the trackway and the odd hoot of an owl.

Felicity wanted to appear calmer than she perhaps felt and did her best to mirror Alex's silence, but there was something bothering her. "What were you doing in the churchyard?"

Alex grimaced. "I could ask you the same thing."

Felicity glowered back at him. "I asked you first."

"Had I not been there, would you have found a way out? Or would you be explaining yourself to the police at this very moment?"

"And what do you think Jasper will say when he finds out you helped me?"

Alex smiled grimly. "Touché. But he won't find out I helped you. Will he?"

Felicity considered the matter for a moment. Rivals or not, she supposed she owed Alex something now.

"Fine. I'll tell you what I was doing in the churchyard. I was following Mr McNabb. He'd been investigating Mr Reeves."

Alex went back to scanning their surroundings. "McNabb is the fellow that got shot, is he?"

As Felicity nodded, her stomach squeezed. It was a disturbing thing to have witnessed, even if she hadn't had a good view of it.

"And he was investigating the murder, was he?"

"No," replied Felicity. "He'd been asking questions around the village before Mr Reeves' death."

Alex lifted his eyebrows. "Really? What was his interest in Reeves?"

"That's just it. I don't know. I'd tried asking him when I saw him at the inn after the memorial service, but he wouldn't tell me."

"How did you know McNabb would be in the churchyard?"

Alex's questions were sharp and quick-fire. Felicity had to be on her guard if she was to keep anything to herself. "I happened to find out he'd be meeting someone who claimed to have information. I wanted to listen in, see what I could learn."

Alex nodded thoughtfully. "Only the person he was meeting clearly had no intention of sharing any information."

Felicity braced herself for a lecture about putting herself in danger, but refreshingly, none came.

"Now it's your turn," she ventured.

"My turn?"

"To tell me what you were doing in the churchyard."

The corner of Alex's mouth lifted into a half smile. "I could tell you, Felicity, but I can guarantee you shan't like it one bit."

"Try me. Please."

"Very well. I was in my room at the inn, working on a story. My typewriter's set up in front of the window with a view of the village, and I don't like to draw the curtains until I go to bed. Everything outside was quiet and still, when something moving out on the village green caught my eye. Imagine my surprise when I looked up and saw Lady Felicity Quick skulking through the shadows and dodging police officers."

Felicity wrinkled her nose. "What's surprising about a local resident walking around the village where she happens to live?"

Alex raised his eyebrows. "In the middle of the night?"

"Certainly," bluffed Felicity. "Why ever not?"

He blinked. "With a murderer on the loose?"

Felicity shrugged nonchalantly, but after what she'd just seen in the churchyard, she was beginning to grasp what Alex and Jasper had meant about a murder investigation being a 'nasty business'.

"Are you intending to write up your late-night visit to the churchyard in the village newsletter?" asked Alex. "Is that what this is about?"

"Actually, no." Felicity took a deep breath. "I quit."

"Aha." Alex was silent for a moment. "Why did you quit, if you don't mind me asking?"

"Editorial differences," said Felicity.

Alex laughed. It was a rich, warm sound, but it wasn't the reaction Felicity had expected. She was somewhat affronted by it.

He shook his head. "If I were to leave my post every time I disagreed with an editor..."

"All right," Felicity said impatiently. "And I suppose you've got further with the story, have you?"

Alex cleared his throat a little. "I've found a few in-roads with the detectives from Exeter. They seem to think the local bobbies might have made a few mistakes early on. They're not thrilled with how they secured the scene of the crime, but we won't print that, of course. It's not exactly good for public confidence."

Felicity nodded knowingly but said nothing.

"They've found the murder weapon now though," continued Alex, "and that's given them more to work with."

Felicity's stomach fell. "It's Lord Northcote's gun, isn't it? They think it's him, don't they?"

"If only it were that simple," Alex said with a sigh. "The man has his wife as an alibi, and apparently, he wasn't too careful about keeping his firearms locked up safely. He had a selection of guns in an outbuilding, which was essentially always left open. I must say, I can understand why the police would be suspicious of him. A spouse is hardly a reliable alibi, and the unlocked outbuilding seems rather convenient given the circumstances."

"Lord Northcote," said Felicity brusquely, "happens to be my Uncle Basil."

Alex glanced at her. "That's funny. Jasper never mentioned that Lord Northcote is a relation of yours."

"He's not a blood relation. He was a very good friend of my father's."

"Does that bring you to the conclusion that Lord Northcote couldn't possibly have done it?"

Felicity looked at Alex, but there was no sign of mockery on his face. It was a genuine question.

"I know Lord Northcote well enough to say he would never resort to murder," said Felicity. "And even if he did — which he absolutely wouldn't, by the way — he'd not leave a mess of it in the village for the locals to find. He's an upstanding member of society. He cares about the local community."

"So if Lord Northcote didn't do it, who did?"

Felicity was quiet for a moment, their footsteps on the trackway the only sounds. She thought about the N she'd seen in the mud, but she wasn't ready to share the information with Alex, or with anyone.

"I thought Mr McNabb might know something about the murder," she said.

"Well, now that he's been shot himself, I'd say your Mr McNabb seems an unlikely suspect. Did you manage to see anything much of who did it?"

Felicity shook her head. "I saw only his feet. Or perhaps her feet."

"Her feet?"

Felicity was thinking of Nora. She'd imagined the little maid incapable of murder, but was it really so hard to fire a gun? Felicity wasn't yet ready to confide this idea in Alex. He'd probably tell her she was being farfetched.

"What did you see?" she asked.

"The same as you," said Alex. "Bit hard to draw any conclusions from a pair of boots."

"The police haven't officially named Lord Northcote as their suspect, have they?"

"No, but if they find more evidence pointing in his direction, they might have to take that step."

Felicity nodded stiffly. "I see."

"I'm sure it doesn't help his case that it's common knowledge Reeves and Lord Northcote had had a falling out," continued Alex, "even if it was only over a garden plant. Several of the villagers I've interviewed mentioned the disagreement to me. On top of that, Lord Northcote won't talk to the newspapers. All the journalists have asked him, and he's turned us all down. It gives the impression he has something to hide."

"Even if he doesn't," said Felicity.

They'd arrived at Oakridge Head. Making up the hamlet were several thatched cottages and a farmhouse whose slate roof shone in the moonlight. Beyond the farmhouse, the trackway forked. In one direction, it led past the fields belonging to Oakridge Farm, winding through a shallow valley towards Sweetbrooke. In the other direction, it climbed a gentle hill and connected with the lane that ran alongside the grounds of Bradley Court.

Felicity stopped walking and folded her arms over her tweed jacket. "You needn't accompany me any further. I know my way from here."

Alex put his hands in his trouser pockets and rocked on his heels. "Do you think I've been accompanying you because I imagined you didn't know your way?"

Felicity tutted. "I can get home safely from here by myself."

Alex looked around at the hamlet and the empty fields beyond. "I can almost accept that." He kicked at a stone with the toe of his shoe. "But I'd feel better if you allowed me to accompany you all the way to Bradley Court. It's safer than travelling by yourself."

"Well," said Felicity, her back straightening. "I'd feel better if you didn't. I've taken up quite enough of your time for one night." *And I stopped needing a nanny many years ago*, she added silently.

Alex narrowed his eyes. "You haven't yet asked me what I've dug up about Reeves. Are you not a little curious to know what I've found?"

There was only a brief pause before Felicity responded. "I might be."

Alex began walking towards Bradley Court. Felicity let out a sigh of defeat and followed him.

"Reeves," began Alex, kicking another stone off the trackway and into the grass, "was potentially involved in a scandal before coming to Lower Diddleton. Did you ever hear about the Dalloway affair?"

Felicity shook her head. "You can go back to Oakridge Head. I know all about the Dalloway affair."

Alex's eyebrows drew low. "How do you know about it? Reeves was never named in the press. Dalloway himself wasn't, for that matter."

"I shan't reveal my sources," Felicity said, happy to have got just as far as her rival in her investigations. "What else do you know?"

Alex sighed. "That's all I have. The newspaper has researchers in Bristol and London poring over the public archives for anything we might unearth about Reeves or any family members. We could get lucky there, but it can take time, and it certainly doesn't help that he seems to have had no living relatives to speak of."

"Will you tell me what you find out?"

Alex smiled and shook his head. "Once you get your teeth in, you don't let go, do you?"

Felicity blinked. She couldn't tell if Alex's remark was complimentary, but he was right. She couldn't let the matter of murder in Lower Diddleton go.

As the whitewashed crenelations of Bradley Court's roof appeared over the crest of the hill, an idea took shape in Felicity's mind.

"I have a proposal," she said.

Alex kicked another stone. "Go on."

"If you still want to speak to Lord Northcote, I can get you an interview with him."

Alex smiled. "And I suppose you want something in return."

Felicity nodded. She wasn't smiling. She was serious.

"What is it?"

"Let me cover the murder story with you. I don't need any credit. I don't need a byline. I just want to be involved."

A deep frown settled on Alex's features. "How could I possibly agree to that? You know how unhappy it would make your brother."

"He was planning for us to work together," pressed Felicity. "He wanted me to shadow you, remember?"

"Not on a murder case."

"Jasper doesn't have to know."

"How do you propose to ensure that?"

"I won't tell him. We can be careful."

"Doesn't mean he won't find out. He's got a nose for these kinds of things. You know that as well as I do."

They walked on in silence. Alex's brow remained furrowed, the scar on his forehead visible. He wasn't keen on her proposal, but he was thinking about it.

Bradley Court's high, arched windows appeared beyond the trees, sparkling in the moonlight. Wind rustled through the hedgerows as they stopped where the trackway from Oakridge Head joined the lane running from Bradley Court to Lower Diddleton.

"So." Felicity looked up at Alex, folding her arms over her chest. "Do we have a deal?"

Chapter Nineteen

SITTINGDON HALL, NEAR LOWER DIDDLETON, EAST DEVON, 13 JUNE 1921

"I can't bear it any longer." Lord Northcote was in Sittingdon Hall's conservatory, but his booming voice thundered through the large, elegantly decorated entrance hall of the stately home. "I'll hand myself in, I tell you. I'll give myself up to the police. That's what they want, isn't it?"

Lady Northcote's gentle tones could be heard soothing Lord Northcote, though her precise words weren't distinguishable, because unlike her husband, she spoke at normal volume rather than shouting.

The inscrutable elderly butler who'd opened Sittingdon Hall's front door to Felicity and Alex cleared his throat. "This way, please." He had perhaps grown used to Lord Northcote's outbursts over the years. Either that or he'd grown deaf.

Crossing the entrance hall, the low heels of her white Mary Janes clicking across the grey marble floor, Felicity turned to Alex. "What you just heard doesn't count," she whispered, wincing inwardly at the terrible impression Lord Northcote was already making. "The interview hasn't started yet."

She had Pip tucked under the arm of her peppermint green sports jacket, with which she was wearing a matching skirt, a white picture hat, and a hand-tooled bag in white leather. The little dog was thankfully more accommodating of Alex's presence than he had been when they'd met at the Cat and Cream. He growled only when making eye-contact with him.

"I'll be as impartial as possible," said Alex, who looked extremely presentable in a dark grey suit with a subtle white check. "But I can't close my ears just because you don't like what's being said. What kind of journalist would that make me?"

Felicity glared at Alex, but stopped short of open disagreement. They were no longer rivals. He'd agreed to allow her to be involved in reporting on the murder, and to keep her part of the deal, Felicity had arranged an interview with Lord Northcote. She'd hoped the interview would help cement Lord Northcote's reputation as an innocent in the whole affair, but her hopes were already dwindling, and Alex had yet to ask him a question.

An ornate Swiss clock mounted on the wall of the entrance hall struck eleven as they arrived in the bright, warm conservatory. It was a relatively recent addition to Sittingdon Hall, jutting out onto the lawn at the back of the house, and Lady Northcote used it to house part of her extensive collection of pelargoniums, which bloomed in white, pink and red. Their leaves added a gentle note of citrus to the air.

"My lord, my lady," began the butler's announcement. "Lady Felicity Quick of Bradley Court and Mr Alexander Cooper of the Western Daily News."

"Thank you, Simmons." Lady Northcote stepped forward to greet Felicity with a kiss on each cheek. Beside her feet was Heather, the aged Cocker Spaniel's tail slowly but enthusiastically beating the air. "Lovely to see you, as always, Felicity. It's a pleasure to meet you, Mr Cooper," she added, holding out a hand to Alex.

"Thank you for welcoming me," said Alex, shaking Lady Northcote's hand. "And for agreeing to the interview."

Lady Northcote rested a hand on her chest. "Oh, no need to thank me, Mr Cooper. Everything was arranged between Felicity and Basil. Basil barely listens to me anymore. Sometimes I rather think I'm here simply to pour the tea. Do you take sugar, by the way?"

Lord Northcote didn't step forward to offer any greeting. Standing with his hands firmly wedged in the waistcoat pockets of his brown suit, he eyed Alex carefully.

Felicity placed Pip on the ground and approached Lord Northcote.

"Uncle Basil," she said, kissing him on the cheek. "Thank you again for agreeing to be interviewed. You shan't regret it, I promise."

"Shan't I?" said Lord Northcote, fixing Alex with another frosty glare.

"Pleased to meet you, my lord." Alex approached Lord Northcote and extended his hand. "It's a privilege to be allowed into your home and to speak to you on behalf of the Western Daily News."

Lord Northcote gave Alex's hand the briefest of shakes. "Shall we get on with it?" he grumbled.

They sat on sturdy wicker furniture, which was padded with thick chintz cushions. As Lady Northcote poured cups of steaming Ceylon, a whine went up from the corner of the conservatory. Pip was making himself comfortable in Heather's basket, turning circles before finally settling, the elderly sad-eyed spaniel looking on in disappointment.

Lord Northcote leaned back in his chair, his hands on the armrests. Alex, who was seated on a sofa next to Felicity, took his notepad from his pocket.

"Ask me then," barked Lord Northcote.

Lady Northcote exchanged a nervous glance with Felicity.

Alex blinked calmly. "Ask you what, my lord?"

"You want to know whether I did it, don't you?"

"Did what?" said Alex innocently.

"Oh, come on. Don't play games. You want to know whether I killed Reeves. That's what you're jolly well here for, isn't it?"

"Now, Basil," began Lady Northcote.

"Very well," said Alex. "Did you do it?"

Felicity looked at Alex with surprise. The bluntness of the question was shocking, even if Lord Northcote had invited it.

Fixing Alex with a look as hard as steel, Lord Northcote said, "If I wanted a man dead, do you think I'd leave his body on the village green for every Tom, Dick, and Harry to gawp at?"

Lady Northcote shook her head, her fingers knotting anxiously in her lap. "Really, Basil. I thought we discussed this already." She turned to Alex with an apologetic smile. "Please don't write that down. My husband doesn't want anyone dead. I promise you he doesn't."

Alex glanced at his notepad. "With all due respect, my lord, that doesn't answer my question."

"Of course I didn't bally do it!" exploded Lord Northcote, spots of red appearing on his cheeks. "What kind of idiot do you take me for? Reeves was a menace, all right, but not worth swinging for."

"And the shooting in the graveyard last night," Alex continued coolly. "Were you involved?"

Felicity sent a remorseful glance towards Lady Northcote, but her frightened eyes were fixed on her husband, evidently terrified of what he might say next. Felicity bit her lip, full of regret. The interview was already a complete disaster.

Lord Northcote's eyebrows drew together. "A shooting in the graveyard? What are you talking about?"

Felicity cleared her throat, happy to interject. "Another man was shot last night, Uncle Basil," she said. "In the grounds of All Angels church."

Lady Northcote lifted a hand to her elegant throat. "Another murder?"

"I didn't even know there'd been another shooting." Lord Northcote threw up a hand and let it land with a *thwack* on the arm of his chair. "How could it have been me if I don't even know it happened? Did they find the weapon yet? Was it another of my guns? If it was, I can tell you that those two gamekeepers of mine are going to get a very stern talking to. Very stern, indeed. Everything is to be kept locked up now. I've made that abundantly clear."

As Lord Northcote spoke, Alex's pencil moved fluidly across the pages of his notebook. From the other end of the sofa, Felicity recognised some symbols from the Pitman shorthand she used herself, but many of the marks were unfamiliar to her, leaving her unable to read his notes. Experienced journalists often developed their own forms of notation, and Alex was certainly experienced.

"Do you know a Mr McNabb, Lord Northcote?" Alex asked.

Even deeper lines appeared on Lord Northcote's forehead. "McNabb? Can't say as I do. Name means nothing to me. Why? Who is he? The fellow that was shot? Dead, is he?"

Alex's tone remained calm and businesslike. "Yes, he's the man that was shot in the churchyard, and no, he's not yet dead."

"They're taking care of him at the Royal Devon and Exeter," said Felicity gently, repeating what Alex had told her earlier that morning, having gleaned the information from his police contacts. "He's badly injured, I'm afraid."

Lady Northcote stared at her hands in her lap. "It's all just so horrible, isn't it?" she said, addressing no one in particular.

"Why do you think people are suspicious of you, Lord Northcote?" pressed Alex.

"Well, I..." Lord Northcote shifted in his seat. "Are people suspicious of me? I mean, I know it was my bally gun, but I already explained all that."

Alex continued making notes as he spoke. "What was your relationship with Reeves like?"

Lord Northcote was quiet for a moment. "The man was a menace," he said steadily. "And I've made no secret of my feelings towards him. But that doesn't mean I killed the fellow, does it?" He turned to Felicity. "Just who is this chap? I thought you said he was one of your brother's star reporters? He doesn't seem particularly bright to me."

Without giving Felicity a chance to respond, Alex continued his questioning. "And the origin of your disagreement with Reeves was what exactly?" He looked at his notebook. "A garden plant?"

"Well." Again Lord Northcote shifted. "Yes."

"Nothing else?"

Felicity turned to Lady Northcote, ready to offer another look of apology for Alex's sharp questions, but Lady Northcote's gaze was concentrated on her husband.

"You may as well tell him everything, Basil," she said.

Lord Northcote eyed Alex for a moment. "All right. Reeves and I had another disagreement. About my staff."

Alex lifted his eyebrows enquiringly.

Lord Northcote huffed. "I never like to get involved in this kind of business, but one of my gamekeepers, Jim Coombe, is uncle to Reeves' maid."

Felicity's eyes widened as she took a sip of tea. The older of Lord Northcote's two gamekeepers had comforted Nora in the church after the memorial service. Knowing that he was her uncle, the scene now made sense.

Lord Northcote continued. "Reeves was unhappy about the time his maid was spending away from his house. She apparently told him she was visiting Sittingdon Hall to see her uncle. Reeves found it unacceptable and came to tell me to keep my staff in order."

"How did you respond?" asked Alex.

"Well, this was after the matter with the poisonous bush, so you can imagine I wasn't best pleased to see Reeves on my doorstep. And as far as my staff are concerned, if they're doing their work and not mixing with individuals of ill repute, then I don't bally care who they see in their spare time. So I told old Reeves there was nothing I would do about it. Ha! You should have seen the man's face."

"Basil," hissed Lady Northcote reprovingly.

Her husband's gleeful smile quickly disappeared from under his moustache. "Listen," Lord Northcote said to Alex. "I didn't like the fellow, it's true, but I still hope they catch whoever did it. Murder isn't ever right, but it's especially wrong in a place like Lower Diddleton."

Alex nodded thoughtfully, looked at his notes, and returned his gaze to Lord Northcote. "Who do you believe killed Reeves?"

Lord Northcote puffed out his cheeks and let out a breath. "I'll be dashed if I know. I suppose Felicity's already told you about the Dalloway affair?"

Alex nodded.

"No one could prove Reeves' involvement, of course," continued Lord Northcote. "But I wonder if Reeves' death isn't somehow related."

Alex took a few more notes. "Will you be at the inquest this afternoon?"

"Not much choice in that. Got to answer a few questions about my gun collection. They can ask me whatever they like, of course. I have a solid alibi." Lord Northcote looked at Lady Northcote. She smiled back at him with a hint of sadness that expressed her longing for this whole messy affair to be over and done with as quickly as possible.

Lady Northcote turned to Alex. "Do you have any further questions, Mr Cooper?"

As Alex flicked through the pages of his notebook, Felicity took the opportunity to become involved. They'd agreed to work together, after all.

Leaning forward, she asked, "Could we have a word with your gamekeepers, Uncle Basil?"

Chapter Twenty

A soft summer breeze blew the scent of sweet peas across the gravel path as Felicity and Alex made their way through Sittingdon Hall's gardens and away from the big house. Pip trotted alongside them, sniffing the grass and occasionally chewing a sprig or two. Birds chirruped in the tall trees that surrounded a group of outbuildings out of sight of the main house. Built in a mix of rough stone and dark timber, the buildings included stabling for horses and were arranged around a cobbled yard.

"I didn't expect Lord Northcote to allow access to his gamekeepers," said Alex as they entered the yard. "But I imagine they'll be tight-lipped. Outdoor workers often are with journalists."

"Perhaps they'll speak off the record?" said Felicity. "We've certainly plenty to ask them, and not just about the murder weapon. I wonder what Coombe might have to say about Mr Reeves, seeing as his niece worked for him."

"Indeed." Alex lifted his eyebrows. "If we can get them to talk, it'll be quite the scoop."

Felicity smiled. "My local contacts have proven useful, then."

Alex turned to her briefly. "Did I ever say they wouldn't?"

The building in which they'd been told they would likely find the gamekeepers — if the two men weren't stalking the grounds of Sittingdon Hall for signs of poachers — was a large shed that had originally been used to keep acorns with which to fatten pigs. The shed had been converted to a workshop and store for the gamekeepers. It was from this building that the gun that killed Mr Reeves had been taken.

Felicity's heels clicked on the cobbles as she and Alex entered the gamekeepers' shed. Open double doors provided most of the light inside, what windows there were being rather sparse and small, leaving the far corners of the space cast in dark shadow. The walls were made from a single layer of tarred oak boards, which gave the interior a strong, musty smell. The atmosphere contrasted starkly with the bright light and sweetly scented air of the June day outside. Pip paused in the shed doorway. Paw lifted, he sniffed the air then trotted away towards the stable block.

At Felicity and Alex's arrival, the younger of the two gamekeepers, who on close inspection appeared to be around twenty years of age, looked up from a heavily scarred wooden workbench positioned in the daylight coming from the shed's entrance. His features were angular, his nose pointed like a hawk's, and his eyes just as piercing. Before him on the bench was a metal rabbit trap, its teeth glinting. In his hands was a thick steel file.

"Can I 'elp you?" The young man spoke gruffly, implying he had no intention of helping anyone.

Felicity smiled politely. "This is Mr Alex Cooper, a journalist from the Western Daily News. I'm Lady Felicity Quick, of Bradley Court. Mr Cooper has just interviewed Lord Northcote, and now, with Lord Northcote's permission, Mr Cooper would like to speak to you."

The young gamekeeper stared at Felicity unflinchingly. His silence in response to her introduction made Felicity uncomfortable, and her smile grew awkward.

"S'all right, Mayhew. You get on with your work." The older gamekeeper stepped out from the shadows at the back of the building. His lined face and discoloured teeth placed him at perhaps fifty years of age, and he carried a shotgun under his arm — pointed, thankfully, at the ground — which he appeared to be in the process of cleaning. "I can answer what questions you have, my lady." Although his words seemed accommodating enough, the older gamekeeper had a hard stare, which was not unlike the younger gamekeeper's. "The name's Jim Coombe. That there's Paul Mayhew. We're the gamekeepers on this here estate. Though I s'pose you know that already."

"Thank you, Mr Coombe," said Felicity with a polite smile, but her uneasiness not quite gone. "Yes, we're aware of the roles played by Mr Mayhew and yourself here on Lord Northcote's estate."

"May we see where the murder weapon was kept?" asked Alex, in what Felicity recognised as his customary direct style of questioning. Alex had his notepad in his hand and was already making notes, his eyes scanning the interior of the shed.

As Coombe led them to the far wall, his gait somewhat bow-legged, Mayhew returned to his work sharpening the teeth of the rabbit trap, the repeated strokes of the metal file creating a rasping and unpleasant rhythm.

"This here is where we keep the shotguns and rifles," said Coombe, pointing towards a tall metal cabinet fixed to the wall with a heavy padlock hanging on the front. As Felicity and Alex inspected the cabinet, the gamekeeper put down the shotgun he'd been holding on a work surface that ran along most of the shed's side wall.

"I see the padlock is new," said Alex, tugging on the shiny metal device. "Did the murderer break the old one?"

The old gamekeeper laughed, a dry, guttural sound. "By Jove, sir. No. There was never a lock on this here cupboard. Only on the shed door."

"So the murderer broke the lock on the shed door?" Alex asked.

Coombe looked across at his younger colleague, but Mayhew didn't look up from the rabbit trap.

"Not exactly, sir," said the old gamekeeper. "And I can only be honest with you, as you'll no doubt hear it at the inquest soon enough. We were in the habit of leaving it open, sir. No breaking in needed. Police weren't too 'appy when they heard that, of course. But that's how it was."

"Who knew there were firearms kept here?" pressed Alex.

"Why, you sound just like one of them police officers, you do." Coombe's smile revealed gaps in a row of unhealthy-looking teeth. "And I'll tell you just what I told them. Common knowledge, it was. Never been a secret that we had guns in here."

Felicity frowned. "Wasn't it rather a risk leaving the place unlocked?"

Coombe folded his arms over his chest. "You're a local maid, aren't you, my lady? When would you say the last time was something 'appened round here like burglary, let alone something like what 'appened to poor old Mr Reeves?"

"Well," said Felicity. "Never."

Coombe lifted his eyebrows at Felicity. "Exactly."

Alex looked around the space. "Where do you and Mr Mayhew sleep?"

"We've rooms above the stables," replied Coombe. "On the other side of the courtyard."

"Did you see or hear anything the night Mr Reeves was killed?" asked Alex.

"No, sir. Sleep like a rock, I do. Work what's physical and has you outside most of the day will do that to a man."

"And Mr Mayhew?" Alex nodded his head towards the younger gamekeeper, who was still at work on the rabbit trap.

"No, sir. He didn't hear nothing neither." Coombe took a step towards Alex and lowered his voice. "And I'd like it if you didn't bother him about it. The police 'ave been here more times than I can count, and there's the inquest this afternoon. A sensitive lad, Mayhew is. Parents both dead. His father was a suicide."

"Terribly sorry to hear that," said Felicity solemnly.

"Took him under my wing, I did," continued Coombe. "Not

been with us long, and I'll not 'ave him upset by all this murder nonsense."

Mayhew remained absorbed in his work on the rabbit trap, his shoulders hunched as he pressed the file onto the teeth. He didn't appear to be a sensitive soul that could be easily upset, but then Felicity wasn't overly familiar with the type of man who worked outdoors for a living and for whom hunting and dealing with animal carcasses was par for the course. Among gamekeepers, Mayhew was perhaps obviously a gentle soul.

"I've no need to speak to Mr Mayhew," said Alex, "so long as you're able to answer my questions, Mr Coombe. Have there been any more guns taken since the murder of Mr Reeves?"

"Oh, I see, sir," said Coombe, rocking back on his heels. "Thinking about that business in the churchyard last night, are you? Ah, yes. Heard all about that, we 'ave. One of the stable boys brought the news from the village. First that Reeves fellow. Now some chap from Scotland, wasn't he? Very nasty business. Very nasty."

"Did any guns go missing last night?" repeated Alex calmly.

"From here, sir? No, there wasn't." Coombe slapped a hand on the tall gun cabinet with a metallic clang. "All kept locked up now. You'd need a stick of dynamite to get in 'ere."

Alex continued writing in his notebook. "Did you hear or see anything last night?"

"No, sir. Like I said, when we sleep, we sleep like the dead. And there was nothing doing up 'ere. They lost the scent of their man out in Venny Woods. Whoever did it didn't come by Sittingdon this time. Got their gun from some place else."

Alex flicked through his notes. Felicity took advantage of the pause in his questioning. "May I ask you about your niece, Mr Coombe?"

The gamekeeper's forehead creased. "What, little Nora?"

"She was Mr Reeves' maid, wasn't she?"

"She was, yes. Poor girl. Very unlucky, she's been. Not nice at all to have your first employer murdered like that. She found it 'ard enough to get a job in the first place. Such a timid thing, she is. It'll be difficult for her to get another position now, with no references."

"I can only imagine," said Felicity sympathetically. "Do you know if Mr Reeves was a good employer? Did Nora like Mr Reeves?"

"I'd say he was a fair employer," said Coombe thoughtfully. Can't say as she liked or disliked him. 'E could be a bit strict over what hours she worked, but never treated her unkindly. She was very upset when he died. Quite a blow for her, it was."

Alex made notes as Felicity continued her questioning.

"Did Nora and Mr Reeves ever have a disagreement of which you're aware?" she asked. "Did your niece ever argue with Mr Reeves?"

Coombe frowned deeply. Then he laughed, a big, booming laugh that filled the shed and took Felicity by surprise. Mayhew looked up from his rabbit trap.

"Forgive me, my lady," said Coombe, wiping his eye on the back of a gnarled finger. "But are you thinking that little Nora might 'ave had something to do with the murder? That's a very amusing idea, that is. Very amusing."

"Did she have something to do with Mr Reeves' death?" asked Alex plainly.

Coombe's face turned instantly serious. "No, sir," he said firmly. "She certainly did not."

"Did you know Mr Reeves, Mr Coombe?" continued Alex.

"No, sir. Saw 'im only a couple of times when visiting Nora, like. Never spoke to the man."

"And did Mr Mayhew have any dealings with Mr Reeves?"

Coombe's chest puffed up. "Here. What's that got to do with anything?"

The scraping of the metal file stopped. "No," said Mayhew, his manner still gruff. He turned to address Alex. "I had no dealings with him."

"S'all right, Mayhew. You get on with things." The older gamekeeper thrust his chin towards Alex. "Will that be all?" he said in a way that implied it would be.

Felicity and Alex were quiet as they left the gamekeepers' shed and rejoined Pip in the cobbled yard. Sawdust, dock burs, and tufts of sheep's wool were entangled in the little dog's fur, which would take some strong brushing to get fully clean, but Felicity didn't chastise Pip. Her mind was far too busy processing the interview with Coombe.

With Pip in the lead, they turned their backs on the cobbled yard and began walking towards Sittingdon Hall. The mansion's honey-coloured sandstone walls rose from the brow of a gentle slope and into the blue sky.

"What do you make of it all?" asked Alex, squinting in the sun as he turned to Felicity, his hands deep in his jacket pockets.

"Well," began Felicity thoughtfully. "Both gamekeepers are no doubt handy with a gun, but what man isn't after the war?"

Alex nodded.

"What I miss," continued Felicity as they climbed the grassy slope, "is motive. What could either of them possibly have against Mr Reeves?"

"Perhaps they felt protective of Lord Northcote?" said Alex. "Or were particularly upset on behalf of the horse that got poisoned? Maybe Coombe didn't like how Reeves was treating his niece?"

"I spoke to Nora at the memorial reception, only very briefly, but she told me Mr Reeves was a good employer. And she was terribly upset during the service."

Alex looked towards Sittingdon Hall. "Which brings us back to Lord Northcote, who's happy to tell anyone who'll listen that Mr Reeves was a menace who won't be missed."

Felicity shot a glare at Alex. "Do you actually think Lord Northcote did it?"

"No," said Alex after a brief pause.

Felicity almost sighed with relief.

"If Lord Northcote had done it," continued Alex, "I believe he'd be smart enough to downplay his disagreements with the dead man, not draw attention to them."

"I hope the police see it that way," said Felicity as they entered the house's parterre gardens. "Don't they have any other suspects?"

"We'll find out more at the inquest," said Alex, side-stepping a mass of bright pink oriental poppies that had sagged onto the path. "You have your suspicions about the maid, though, don't you?"

Felicity drew her eyebrows together. "It's far-fetched, I know."

"It's not a completely ridiculous idea," retorted Alex. "Domestics murder their employers all the time. Well, perhaps not all the time, but often enough for such deeds not to be unheard of."

Felicity swallowed. An excited sort of nervousness rose in her chest as they arrived on Sittingdon Hall's paved terrace. She bent down and scooped Pip under her arm, stroking his little head. "Should we interview Nora Andrews?"

"She'll speak at the inquest, no doubt. Let's see what she has to say to the coroner, and decide what to do after that." Alex looked at his wristwatch, his lightly pomaded dark-blond hair shining in the sun, the scar on his forehead just noticeable. "If I'm to walk to the village, then I need to leave now. I have copy to work on over lunch, before the inquest starts."

There was little risk of Lord or Lady Northcote sharing news of Felicity and Alex's collaboration with Jasper, as Jasper neglected his social obligations to practically everyone since becoming editor-in-chief of the family newspaper, but Felicity and Alex couldn't risk their association with one another becoming common knowledge in the village. They'd therefore agreed to travel to and from Sittingdon Hall separately.

"We could run you down to the edge of the village?" suggested Felicity. "Finnegan wouldn't breathe a word of it to anyone. He's extremely discreet."

Alex shook his head. "I could do with the walk. Help me get my thoughts in order."

Seated in the back of the Rolls, Pip on her lap, Finnegan at the wheel, Felicity watched the countryside whizz by as the breeze played with her curls. They passed Alex striding along the dappled shade of the lane leading to the village. Again, her stomach squeezed with a little burst of excitement. Whether she received credit for her work with Alex didn't matter. She was back on the story. She was reporting on the murder in Lower Diddleton.

Chapter Twenty-One

"Felicity dear, shall we travel together to the Cat and Cream for the inquest?"

Lady Henrietta peered at her granddaughter as the footman cleared away the glasses from which they had just enjoyed a post-lunch dessert of syllabub flavoured with orange blossom.

"Well," began Felicity thoughtfully, as Pip, who was curled asleep on her lap, issued a rather heavy snore.

Thankfully, Jasper was back in Bristol on newspaper business. Still, throughout lunch, Felicity had been trying to think of an excuse that would allow her to go into Lower Diddleton to attend the inquest without prompting too many questions from Lady Henrietta. As it turned out, she needn't have bothered.

"You mustn't take notes or interview anyone, naturally," continued Lady Henrietta. "Jasper wouldn't be at all pleased about that. But I somehow feel it wouldn't be right for no Quick to be present." Lady Henrietta's lavender eyes gleamed as they often did when she partook in gossip, meaning it was unlikely to be family duty alone behind her drive to attend the inquest. "Wouldn't you agree, dear?"

Felicity nodded decisively. "You're absolutely right, Grandmama. I'd be happy to escort you."

After careful relocation of Pip to a sunlit chaise longue in the drawing room, where he could snore to his heart's content while disturbing precisely no one, Felicity and her grandmother arrived at the Cat and Cream with plenty of time to spare ahead of the inquest's official start and were directed to the inn's dining room, which was quickly filling with people.

"It seems busier than the memorial service," hissed Lady Henrietta.

"The press and police are all here, too," replied Felicity, scanning the inn's low-ceilinged dining room as they shuffled towards the last empty seats.

The tables had been pushed to the walls, and the chairs had been repositioned into audience rows facing the coroner's table. Local people filled most of the seats, the police officers watching from the sides of the room with solemn faces, but one section of the seating had been reserved for members of the press. Sure enough, Alex was there, nodding thoughtfully as a fellow journalist spoke animatedly beside him, but Felicity didn't allow her gaze to linger. They'd agreed not to exhibit signs of camaraderie towards one another in Lower Diddleton, as neither wanted word getting back to Jasper.

Felicity and her grandmother took their seats. Wearing an inappropriately loud yellow and grey suit, Mr Chesterton loitered obsequiously beside the table behind which the coroner was seated, the thrill of seeing his dining room so full of people clearly legible on his face. The coroner was a large bespectacled man of between fifty and sixty years of age. When he announced the beginning of the proceedings, Mr Chesterton withdrew to the side of the room, and silence fell as the first witnesses were called to give evidence.

The early testimonies were mostly formal and predictable. They distinctly lacked in the excitement for which many in the audience were undoubtedly waiting. When a doctor from Sweetbrooke, who'd been the first medical professional to arrive on the scene, told the coroner that there'd been nothing he could have done to help Mr Reeves, Lady Henrietta rolled her eyes.

"Of course he couldn't have helped him," she whispered to Felicity. "The man was dead."

When Sergeant Hodgkins sat before the coroner to explain how he and Constable Price had preserved the scene of the crime, Felicity bit her lip, but after more than an hour of dry, rather obvious statements, the audience was fidgeting in their seats. The most interesting witnesses were the police officer who had found the discarded murder weapon — in a field past the hamlet of Ashstone, which was new information for Felicity — and the pathologist who had performed the autopsy on Mr Reeves' body.

"The victim was shot from the front and died of a gunshot wound to the chest," said the coroner. "Is that correct?"

The pathologist nodded. "That is correct."

"And the injury was consistent with that one would expect from the double-barrelled rifle the police found?"

"Indeed. It's a rather uncommon weapon. Used mostly overseas for big game."

"Did the victim die instantaneously?"

"No. He didn't. The bullet passed through his lung and a major artery in his chest. Losing blood in his chest collapsed his undamaged lung. He had mud on his hands and on the knees of his trousers, consistent with crawling along the ground. He also had a great deal of mud under his fingernails."

Felicity shifted in her seat. She was likely the only person at the inquest who understood the full significance of the mud under Mr Reeves' fingernails, and the knowledge weighed on her like a granite boulder.

After the pathologist's statements, there came a break during which tea, coffee, and biscuits were served, and the audience took the opportunity to stretch their legs. Felicity glanced at Alex as he stood alone on the other side of the room, but he didn't look up from his notepad, in which he was scribbling rather furiously. Felicity wanted to ask him what he'd understood to be important from the inquest's first session, but of course, she couldn't.

After the break, the coroner called Mrs Winterpole and Father

Neil forward for their testimonies on the discovery of the body. Responding to the question of who heard or saw anything on the night of the murder, both cited the thunderstorm that had lingered above Lower Diddleton for a good portion of the night as the reason no one had been immediately alerted to the shooting at the heart of the village.

"Besides," added Mrs Winterpole. "It's not unusual to hear a gun go off now and then. When one lives in the countryside, one gets quite used to it."

When it came to Lord Northcote's turn to answer the coroner, Felicity sat up straighter in her seat. Alex and the rest of the journalists were watching the proceedings with elevated interest. Although the police had yet to announce it officially, Lord Northcote was the closest anyone had to a suspect.

"Basil looks terribly flustered," hissed Lady Henrietta. "Though I must say, he's never been terribly good at first impressions."

The coroner's questions focused on the guns kept on the grounds of Sittingdon Hall and the rifle believed to be the murder weapon that had been found by the police. Despite his agitated air, Lord Northcote answered the coroner's questions factually and without his usual bluster. He also succeeded in expressing not even a hint of animosity towards the murdered man.

"Would you not agree," said the coroner, "that it was rather negligent to have left the guns as accessible as they were?"

"Crime wasn't much of an issue in Lower Diddleton," said Lord Northcote in a submissive tone Felicity hadn't heard him use before. "But they're all locked up now."

Though no questions were asked about Lord Northcote's disagreements with Mr Reeves — as the inquest was to establish the how of Mr Reeves' death rather than the why — a murmur went around the inn's dining room as Lord Northcote left the witness chair, which testified to the interest in him.

The focus on Sittingdon Hall continued as the gamekeeper, Jim Coombe, was summoned. He confirmed that the rifle the police had found, which was brought forward for display by a white-gloved officer, belonged to the collection kept in the gamekeepers' shed. He also attested that at the time of the murder, both the gun cupboard and the shed had been unlocked.

"Could someone from outside Lord Northcote's estate have had access?" asked the coroner.

"Oh, yes, sir. There's walls and fences, of course, but they're to keep the animals in, not to keep people out."

"Are the boundaries of Lord Northcote's estate patrolled?"

"No, sir. Never been a reason for it. Not till now."

Felicity scanned the crowd, but Mayhew, the younger of the two gamekeepers, wasn't present. No doubt the protective Coombe had something to do with that. It wasn't difficult to imagine either of the two gamekeepers, with their stony stares and proximity to death, levelling one of their guns at another human, but then neither of their names began with N, and as Alex had said, what was their motive?

There came another break. Returning to the packed dining room after a quick trip to the powder room, Felicity again glanced over at Alex. This time, he returned her gaze with a subtle lift of his eyebrows. Mr Reeves' maid, Nora Andrews, was taking the witness chair.

Chapter Twenty-Two

Nora sat meekly before the coroner, her legs crossed at the ankles and her hands together in her lap. Her brown eyes were wide and fearful, and she swept nervously at her fringe, which tickled her forehead from under a navy blue hat. Her jacket was a matching shade of navy, and the skirt underneath was grey.

"You were the maid-of-all-work at Mr Reeves' cottage, were you not?"

Nora's answer was a mumble.

"Speak up, please Miss Andrews," said the coroner impatiently. "What was your answer?"

"Yes, sir. I was."

"There were no other domestics in Mr Reeves' employ?"

"N-no, sir. There were not."

"To your knowledge, Miss Andrews," said the coroner, "was your employer in fear for his life?"

Nora paused. "Not to my knowledge, sir, no."

"Was he in good spirits in the days before his death? Not frightened or worried?"

Nora shook her head. "He was quite normal, sir."

"And what, Miss Andrews, do you mean by 'normal'?" The

coroner peered at the girl over his spectacles. He seemed to have less patience for her than for the other witnesses.

"By normal, I mean..." Nora glanced around her at the rows of packed seats. "By normal, I mean he wasn't worried, sir. He was relaxed, sir. He did his usual activities."

"And what were his 'usual activities'?"

"Mr Reeves spent a lot of time in the garden, sir." Nora sniffed. "He had a lot of plants to tend to. He also wrote and received letters, and walked at least twice a day."

"It was on one of these walks that your employer met his end, was it not?"

Nora nodded.

"Was Mr Reeves in the habit of walking in the dark and in the rain?"

The maid sniffed again. "It wasn't a habit, sir, no, but it wasn't the first time. He'd go when the mood took him."

The coroner glanced at his notes. "Are you aware of anyone who wished Mr Reeves ill?"

"Wished him ill, sir?"

"Wanted to harm him. Had he received threats, for example?"

Nora's fingers knitted together. "Not that I know of, sir."

The coroner sighed. "Your employer being murdered must have come as quite a shock to you, Miss Andrews."

Her voice shrank as she answered. "That's right, sir. Yes."

The coroner made a few more notes and dismissed Nora. She'd been the inquest's last witness. While Nora had said little, she'd said enough to give Felicity the very distinct impression that something was worrying Nora, something perhaps beyond the fact that her employer had been killed. Had Alex noticed Nora's behaviour and considered it suspicious? Felicity glanced at the press section, but Alex had his dark blond head down over his notebook.

Without calling another break, and based on the evidence presented, the coroner ruled Mr Reeves' death to have been caused by deliberate and unlawful killing. Naturally, this came as a surprise to precisely no one, but the pronouncement was still monumental.

Lady Henrietta sighed. “It’s now official. There’s been a murder in Lower Diddleton. I never thought I’d live to see such a day.”

Before the audience stood up, Mr Chesterton leapt before the coroner’s desk. “Refreshments are now being served,” he said in a loud, nasally voice, “if you’d like to come through to the bar area.”

Felicity found it a shame that Michael Chesterton’s name didn’t begin with an N, because it would have made the murder case rather straightforward. The Cat and Cream had so far profited the most from Mr Reeves’ death.

As villagers, police, and journalists alike filed towards the bar, Alex stood to one side, talking to one of the police officers, his notepad at the ready. Felicity wanted quite desperately to speak with him, because their next move was obvious. They had to talk to Nora, but there was no way they could do so together. Felicity wanted to propose that she should carry out the interview alone, as it would be less intimidating than an interview with a journalist from London.

She scanned the dining room for a sign of the maid’s navy hat and began joining the throng of people heading towards the bar. It wasn’t possible to discuss the plan with Alex, but Felicity didn’t want to miss her chance with Nora. She was halted when Lady Henrietta put a hand on Felicity’s elbow, her nose wrinkling as people filed past, chattering about what they’d all heard during the inquest and what sort of biscuits they hoped Mr Chesterton had laid out for them in the bar.

“If you’re staying for tea, Felicity, don’t let me stop you,” said Lady Henrietta. “But I’m going back to Bradley Court. I’ve heard quite enough about bodies and weapons and autopsies for one day. I’ll send Finnegan back down to collect you.”

“No need,” said Felicity, craning her neck as she glimpsed what could have been Nora’s navy blue hat disappearing into the bar. “I’ll walk back. The weather’s nice enough.” She was keen to keep her afternoon as free as possible.

Lady Henrietta raised an eyebrow. “Remember, Felicity. No interviews, and no note-taking. We don’t need to upset Jasper any further. He has an awful lot to worry about, running the newspaper as he does. Kingsley never used to be so hands-on, but I suppose times change." She tugged at the collar of Felicity's peppermint sports jacket. "And do make sure you keep some kind of cover over your neck. It's such a shame you got your lovely curls cut so short. If you're not careful, you'll end up tanned like a farmhand."

"Yes, Grandmama," said Felicity distractedly, concerned she was losing Nora.

As Lady Henrietta made her way towards the exit, Felicity hastened after Nora, when again a hand touched her elbow.

"What is it now?" said Felicity impatiently as she turned, expecting to see her grandmother, but standing before her was Alex, an oddly self-satisfied smile on his face.

"What are you doing?" hissed Felicity. "We agreed not to speak to one another in the village."

Alex turned away from Felicity and put his hands in his pockets, as though it were simply a coincidence that they were standing next to one another. "McNabb has regained consciousness," he said in a low voice, his cleanly shaven jaw barely moving as he spoke. "I'm going to the hospital to see if I can get an interview with him."

"I thought we would speak to Nora?"

"What's more valuable for the newspaper's readership? Do you want us to lose the scoop on McNabb?"

Felicity looked towards the door leading to the bar. Then she looked at Alex. "Fine." He had a point about the scoop on Mr McNabb. The interview with Nora could wait. "I'm coming with you."

Alex twisted towards Felicity, surprised. Quickly, he corrected his stance so that he was again looking away from her. "No. We can't do that. I told you because I thought you'd want to know. I wasn't inviting you along."

Felicity lifted her eyebrows. "We're working together, remember? Besides, you need me there. You go in hard, and I'm there to soften them up."

Alex frowned. "You told me McNabb wouldn't speak to you."

Felicity smiled slyly. "He will this time."

Chapter Twenty-Three

Felicity and Alex left the Cat and Cream separately, Felicity via the main entrance on the village high street and Alex via the door from the dining room leading into the cobbled courtyard. When Felicity arrived at the back of the inn, she was careful to check there was no one watching her before opening the door of a dark green Model T, behind the steering wheel of which Alex sat waiting.

"Is this yours?" asked Felicity, settling into the front passenger seat.

"I borrowed it." Swiftly and efficiently, Alex reversed the vehicle onto the lane at the back of the inn. "It was a swap for a couple of tips about the Reeves story."

Felicity regretted having chosen to sit in the front of the motor. She pulled her white picture hat down and did her best to sink back into her seat, in case they passed anyone she knew. "You've been giving away our hard work," she said irritably. "How will the Western Daily News scoop anyone now?"

Alex smiled as he began guiding the motor along a narrow, bumpy lane, avoiding the village high street. "The motorcar belongs to a journalist from one of the London papers. He got here just this morning. I didn't tell him anything everyone isn't already aware of, only he doesn't know that."

The road surface smoothed out, and Alex brought the motor up to speed. Soon they were whizzing past meadows and hedgerows, going faster than Finnegan ever did in the Rolls. With the windows unlatched, Felicity enjoyed the breeze on her face and the grassy scent of the fields, which stretched to the horizon in undulating shades of green.

"You like it here, don't you?" asked Alex above the sound of the roaring motor.

"What," replied Felicity, "in Devon, you mean?"

Alex nodded.

"Well, yes. Of course. Why wouldn't I?"

"Not everyone is keen on where they come from. It is beautiful here, I suppose."

Felicity lifted her brow. "You suppose?"

Alex smiled. "I take that back. It is beautiful here, most definitely."

They sat in silence, the motor humming as they passed trees and cottages. At a bend in the road, a cloud of starlings lifted off from the ground.

"Will you be staying here for very long?" asked Felicity.

"It's a trial period," said Alex. "Jasper's made it clear he's keen for me to stay, but I'm not sure if I'm ready to leave London yet. If I like it here, I'll stay. If not, I'll go back to the city. The paper I used to work for on Fleet Street has said they'll take me back if I change my mind."

Felicity nodded and considered Alex's situation. "I'm not sure I could live in a place like London."

"Why not?"

She wrinkled her nose. "The dirt, the noise, the constant hustle and bustle." She turned to Alex. "Need I go on?"

"You get used to it after a while." He took his eyes off the road to glance at Felicity. "Plenty of interesting work for a journalist."

"More murder investigations, you mean?"

"Certainly, but that's not all. There are several women working as reporters on Fleet Street now. I haven't come across any working for the local papers down here." He glanced again at Felicity. "Except for you, of course."

"Please," said Felicity, putting her elbow on the passenger door and her fingers to her temple. "Don't torment me. Jasper's not happy with me at all. I sincerely doubt I have any kind of future in newspaper journalism now."

Alex pressed his lips together. "Hmm. I didn't know you were the type to give up easily."

Felicity looked at him sternly. "I'm not."

"Then why let your brother's decisions dictate the direction your life is to take?"

She sighed. "I mean no offence, but you're not exactly from a family like ours. And even if you had an older brother, I doubt he'd ever dream of making decisions on your behalf." Felicity looked out the window. "While I appreciate the encouragement, I don't expect you can truly understand my situation."

"I don't have any brothers," said Alex. "But I had a father who desperately wanted me to join the family business, and I had to let him down. That wasn't easy."

"How so?"

Alex's hands tightened on the wheel. "I come from a family of greengrocers. My father and his father before him. They ran a stall at Covent Garden market. I tried it. Believe me, I did, but it just wasn't for me. All I wanted was to write for the newspapers. Even from when I was very young." Alex glanced at Felicity. "Once you get a taste for it, it never leaves you, does it?"

Felicity shifted on the passenger seat of the Model T, staring at the fields as they flew by. "No," she said thoughtfully. "I don't suppose it does."

"Then we understand one another," said Alex. "Even if just a little."

Felicity looked at him. "Yes," she said. "I suppose we do."

With the square towers of the city's cathedral visible in the distance, Felicity and Alex stopped to ask directions for the Royal Devon and Exeter. After two wrong turns, they pulled up in front of the attractive yet imposing red-brick building that housed Devon's largest hospital. Approaching its entrance, they passed nurses in high-necked uniforms, a series of wooden benches occupied by convalescing patients, and several large terracotta containers overflowing with purple petunias.

"How did you find out about Mr McNabb waking up?" Felicity asked.

"A contact with the Exeter police," said Alex. "New recruits are usually the most eager to share what they know. Gives them a sense of importance."

Felicity nodded. She still had her notebook in her pocket and would have liked to have jotted down Alex's advice, but she didn't want him to think she was a complete novice.

They asked at the front desk where they might find the intensive care ward, and after Felicity convinced the receptionist that she already knew Mr McNabb and that he would be pleased to have her and Alex for company, him being so far away from his native Scotland, they were instructed to follow signs for the Clarke Wing. After a series of twists and turns that led them along brightly lit passages with squeaky linoleum floors, Felicity and Alex reached a desk behind which sat a nurse, her white folded hat dipped over paperwork. The clock on the wall behind her said it was almost five o'clock.

"Good afternoon," said Alex. "We're here to visit Mr Alistair McNabb."

The nurse, a woman of around forty with a plump face and a button nose, fixed Alex with dark, shining eyes. "And you are?"

"Alex Cooper, journalist with the Western Daily News."

The nurse squinted at Alex as though the answer was not the one she wanted to hear.

Felicity quickly intervened. "I'm Lady Felicity Quick, of Bradley Court, near Lower Diddleton. Mr McNabb was a guest in our village, and we'd like very much to see him and lift his spirits. Mr McNabb and I are already acquainted, and I can imagine that as a visitor to Devon, he hasn't any friends or family nearby."

The nurse's face softened a little. "Well, he's still rather weak, but I can let Mr McNabb know you're here. He's indeed not had any visitors since arriving with us."

As the nurse left her seat at the desk and rustled down the corridor in her starched uniform, Alex shook his head and put his hands in his pockets. "Do that often, do you?"

Felicity blinked. "Do what?"

He smiled a little. "Mention that you're Lady Felicity Quick of Bradley Court. I thought you preferred just Felicity."

She shrugged. "I'm not lying to people. That's who I am. Does marching up to strangers telling them you're a newspaper journalist usually work for you?"

Alex lifted his eyebrows in amusement. "Sometimes. It's not a lie."

The nurse returned. "He'll see you, my lady," she said with a cursory glance in Alex's direction. "This way, please."

They arrived in a pale-green room with a small, high window through which a patch of sunlight shone. Mr McNabb lay in the only bed in the room, on a narrow mattress under crisp, white sheets. His skin was sallow, and he looked much older than Felicity had remembered. His moustache, no longer waxed, was rather fluffy, and his right shoulder was thick with bandages.

The nurse stood to one side as Felicity and Alex entered the room. "I'll be back in ten minutes. Can't leave you any longer than that, I'm afraid. Our patient needs his rest."

As the nurse retreated, gently pulling the door to leave it ajar, Felicity took the only chair in the room, next to Mr McNabb's bed, while Alex remained standing. The cool grey-blue of Mr McNabb's eyes switched between Felicity and Alex. He didn't look pleased to see them, but this didn't ruffle Felicity in the slightest. After having been shot, how pleased could one feel about anything?

"I know why you two are here." Mr McNabb's Scottish burr was gravelly. "And it's not to lift my spirits."

Felicity drew her eyebrows together. "We didn't have time to bring you a gift, but I'd like to lift your spirits if I can, Mr McNabb."

"Well, you can't." The Scotsman glared at Alex. "And I certainly don't want to be in the newspapers."

"Fine," assured Alex, sliding his notebook back into the inside pocket of his jacket without a hint of disappointment. "Anything you tell us shall be off the record."

"What happened last night, Mr McNabb?" asked Felicity. "Who was it who shot you?"

Mr McNabb shook his head slowly. "Do you not think he'd have been arrested by now if I knew? It was a man in tweeds with a cap pulled down over his eyes. I saw him only for a second before the gun went off. The first shot missed, thank Heavens. The second one got me in the shoulder."

"Do you think the shooter was trying to kill you?" asked Felicity.

"I would say I'm lucky to be alive. Wouldn't you say so as well?"

"Why would someone want to kill you?" said Alex.

Mr McNabb winced in pain as he shook his head. "Haven't a clue."

"What were you doing in Lower Diddleton?" asked Alex.

"I'm a friend of Lord Dalloway's. Or rather, I was, till the poor man passed."

Felicity sat up straighter. "That's why you were asking about Mr Reeves around the village. There's a connection, isn't there?"

Mr McNabb nodded with difficulty. "I used to be Chief Superintendent for the Edinburgh police division. I'm retired now, but I agreed to look into Reeves for Lord Dalloway's family."

"What was the connection exactly?" asked Alex.

"Blackmail," said Mr McNabb.

Felicity lifted her eyebrows. The pieces of the puzzle were slowly coming together. "Mr Reeves was a blackmailer?"

"He tried it with Lord Dalloway," said Mr McNabb, "but Lord Dalloway refused to pay. That's how he found himself in the papers."

"Why did Dalloway's family want someone looking into Reeves?" asked Alex.

"Did they want revenge?" suggested Felicity, her mind working through the possibilities.

Mr McNabb hesitated, then nodded.

"Did they have Reeves murdered?" asked Alex bluntly.

"Of course not," spluttered the Scotsman. He winced in pain.

"What then?" pressed Alex.

"I was tasked with digging something up on the man."

"To give the blackmailer a taste of his own medicine?" suggested Felicity.

"Exactly that," said Mr McNabb, a gleam in his eye.

"What did you find?" Alex asked.

Mr McNabb sighed. "Sadly, not a lot. Nothing incriminating, at least. The hope had been to find proof he was a blackmailer, but Reeves was good at tidying up after himself. I'd been trying to find others who'd fallen victim to Reeves' little scheme. He would use his access as an accountant to uncover 'irregularities' with which he'd blackmail people. Seems he built up quite a network of informants with contacts he made during the war, accountants and other professionals with access to sensitive personal information. I'd been working on it for many months. I approached people up and down the country, but no one would offer proof of Reeves' blackmailing."

"Why not?" asked Alex.

"It's not unusual for victims of blackmail to not come forward," said Mr McNabb. "That's what makes blackmail so effective. They can be afraid of repercussions from the blackmailer, or deeply ashamed of whatever it is the blackmailer has on them."

"So, as a last resort," said Felicity, "you came to Lower Diddleton to get closer to Mr Reeves."

The Scotsman smiled weakly. "You're a smart one, my lady. Only I didn't have time to do my digging. I arrived in the village, and two days later he was dead."

"I realise you weren't directly involved, but do you think your arrival might have somehow triggered Mr Reeves' murder?" asked Felicity.

Mr McNabb shook his head thoughtfully. "I don't see how."

"When you went to the meeting in the churchyard," said Alex, "who did you expect to see?"

"Someone left a note for me at the inn. No one at the inn saw it being delivered. A rather strange thing, if I'm honest, with the letters cut out of newspaper. I wish I still had it. I'm sure the police would find it interesting."

Felicity reached into her white leather bag, pulled out the note she'd found on the floor at the inn, and held it out to Mr McNabb. His eyes widened. He couldn't move enough to take the paper from her, so she left it resting on his bedsheets. In returning the note to its rightful owner, Felicity felt lighter.

Mr McNabb looked from the note to Felicity. "W-where did you...?"

"I found it on the floor at the inn. I thought it might be significant, so I kept it."

Alex glanced at Felicity and shook his head slowly, a smile playing on his lips.

Felicity cleared her throat, returning her attention to Mr McNabb. "But you have no idea who might have left the note for you?"

"I'd been asking around the village about Reeves. I assumed it would be a local person wanting to share some information with me. The anonymity of the note made me think it might be a victim of blackmail, given the sensitivities around such matters. I had no reason to imagine someone wished me harm."

"Why did someone shoot you, do you think?" asked Alex.

Mr McNabb shifted position and winced. "I can't puzzle it out. If it was the same person who shot Reeves, why shoot me? Wouldn't we have been on the same side? And why in the middle of the village, with all those police around?"

There was silence as the three of them considered the questions to which none of them had any answer.

"Why are you happy to speak to us now," said Alex, "but you didn't want to talk to Lady Felicity at the inn?"

Mr McNabb's face grew grim. "I hadn't been shot yet. It gives a person another perspective on matters." He twisted his head stiffly to look down at his injured shoulder for a moment. "I sincerely hope they catch him. Whoever it is must be a madman. There's no other explanation for such a daring, careless act. Anyone could be next. You should be very careful indeed, my lady."

As Mr McNabb stared at Felicity with foreboding, the starched rustle of the nurse's uniform could be heard returning along the corridor.

"Thank you for everything you've told us, Mr McNabb," said Felicity, a little unsettled. "Your name won't appear in the newspaper, but the information you've shared with us will help us piece together the story people need to read."

Alex cocked a slightly reproving eyebrow at Felicity. Perhaps he'd have preferred to close the interview, but Felicity was quite certain Alex wouldn't have been allowed any time at all with Mr McNabb if she'd not been with him.

"Please," said Mr McNabb. "Do be careful."

There was a gentle tap at the door.

"That was ten minutes," said the nurse. "Goes quickly, doesn't it?"

Chapter Twenty-Four

Felicity stared out of the window as Alex steered the borrowed Model T through the outskirts of Exeter. The edges of the city didn't look enormously dissimilar to Lower Diddleton, except the gardens of the thatched cottages had been much reduced in size, and large, red-brick Victorian villas had been crammed between them. Besides the sound of the engine, their journey so far had mostly been in silence.

"It's a good question," said Alex, somewhat cryptically.

Felicity, however, was on precisely the same page. "Why shoot McNabb, you mean?"

"Yes." Alex glanced at her. "Exactly."

"What do you make of Mr McNabb's assessment? Do you believe the murderer to be a madman?"

"In a community like Lower Diddleton?" Alex frowned. "I don't think a lunatic would go unnoticed. Whoever it is, he's composed enough to keep control of himself. He's able to present himself as a respectable, law-abiding person."

Felicity nodded as the road passed through a grassy common. "You're absolutely right. A maniac doesn't shoot someone in the middle of the village green and get away with it. There's some calculation and skill involved. But do you think it was the same person who shot Mr McNabb as shot Mr Reeves?"

"The chances of there being one murderer in a place like Lower Diddleton are already remote," said Alex, slowing the motor to allow a gaggle of white geese to cross the road, honking as they went. "What would be the chances of two?"

"If whoever shot Mr McNabb also shot Mr Reeves, then what's the person's motive?" Felicity turned to Alex. "Like Mr McNabb said, surely he and whoever did away with Mr Reeves were united in their desire to mete out some kind of punishment for the man, even if their methods differed."

Alex was quiet for a moment. "Unless McNabb killed Reeves, and whoever shot McNabb sought revenge for Reeves."

Felicity squinted at Alex. "You just said the chances of two murderers were slim to none."

"I said it was remote, not impossible."

"And imagine, please, that you're Mr McNabb, and you've just arrived in an unfamiliar village and shot one of its residents dead. Would you attend the man's memorial service before making your getaway? Not to mention show up for a midnight meeting with a stranger in the local churchyard after receiving an anonymous note?"

"That's how you knew to be at the churchyard, wasn't it?"

"What?"

The motor stopped at a junction. Alex glanced at Felicity before returning his eyes to the road. "The note you gave back to McNabb in the hospital just now. The one you found on the floor at the inn." He looked at her again, a little smile on his lips. "At least, that's your story."

Felicity span towards Alex. "What are you suggesting? That I took the note? That I'm a thief?"

He shrugged. "I know what it's like to get completely hooked on a story. There are things a journalist can do that aren't exactly illegal, but aren't exactly morally sound, either."

Felicity scoffed. "What are you talking about? I would never steal."

"Well, you didn't steal it in the end. You gave it back, so technically, you borrowed it."

Felicity sighed deeply and folded her arms over her chest. "I'm not even going to comment on that," she said and looked out the window to distract herself from how frustrating Alex was being.

It wasn't long before he broke the silence. "So, who do you think the murderer is?"

Felicity left a long pause before answering. "I don't know, but I don't believe Mr McNabb had anything to do with Mr Reeves' death."

"That sounds rather similar to your convictions about Lord Northcote's innocence."

Felicity stopped herself from yet again jumping to Uncle Basil's defence, but she was beginning to see how working with another journalist could be infuriating and enlightening in equal measures. "As a matter of fact, I still think we should speak to Nora."

Alex glanced at her, his brow knitted. "You think the maid did it?"

"Not necessarily," said Felicity coolly. "It's not our job to solve the case, anyway. It's our job to report on it."

Alex nodded in agreement. "You're right there."

"I think she might add to the picture we have of Mr Reeves."

The motor passed over a narrow bridge, its rough blocks of grey granite sparkling in the sun and the clear waters of Ridgestone Brook rushing underneath.

"We still have researchers at the paper investigating Reeves' background," said Alex. "It's all been pretty dry up till now, but I can urge them to dig deeper, try to get someone to go on record about Reeves being a blackmailer. Perhaps people are more willing to talk now he's dead."

"Maybe Nora could help us with that?"

Alex shook his head doubtfully. "She seems too naïve to even know how blackmail works, let alone be wise to the fact her employer was at it."

"Well." Felicity fixed her eyes on the road ahead. "We shan't know that for certain unless we speak to her."

Felicity alighted from the Model T on a quiet, gently sloping lane shaded with oaks, just a short walk from Lower Diddleton. She and Alex would re-enter the village separately, Felicity on foot and Alex in the borrowed motor.

They'd agreed on a plan. Alex would get the latest updates from his police contacts and the Western Daily Press's researchers before starting work on the copy that needed to be turned in for the newspaper's morning edition. Meanwhile, Felicity would speak to Nora. Since they couldn't interview her together, Alex had made Felicity promise she wouldn't enter Mr Reeves' cottage, and that she'd talk to Nora at the door, which was visible from the village green. The request amused Felicity, as Alex had been dismissive of the idea that Nora might be involved in her employer's death, but she agreed to it. After the incident in the churchyard, Felicity was becoming wiser to the dangers that came with reporting on a murder.

To exchange information, she and Alex would meet at the back of the inn towards seven o'clock, as it was usually quiet and there were several motors parked there that would offer them shelter from prying eyes. Alex could then include whatever Felicity had gleaned from Nora in his article to be submitted that evening.

As Felicity walked towards the village, swallows flew low across the road's surface, their bubbling chatter filling the air. The pointed grey steeple of All Angels church appeared from behind the treetops, visible against the blue June sky. The bells were ringing six o'clock, and Felicity could imagine her grandmother's concern at her skipping both teatime and dinner, not to mention Pip's indignation at being left alone for practically the whole day. Still, she kept course towards the village. With two journalists working on the story, the Western Daily News had a better chance of getting a scoop and selling more copies, and that would surely make both her grandmother and Jasper happy in the end.

Coming up the lane towards Felicity was a diminutive figure whose identity was obscured by a wide-brimmed straw hat. As they drew closer to one another, the straw hat tipped back to reveal the smiling face of Mrs Winterpole. She had on a brown woollen suit and stout walking shoes.

“There’s nothing quite like a stroll before dinner, is there, Lady Felicity?”

Felicity smiled politely, inwardly thankful that Mrs Winterpole didn’t even think to question what Felicity was doing marching along one of Lower Diddleton’s more obscure thoroughfares, quite on the opposite side of the village to Bradley Court. “Indeed, Mrs Winterpole. I can only agree.”

“Rain or shine, I always take a walk before dinner.” Mrs Winterpole drew in a deep breath. “Fresh air and the exercise do one the world of good. My maid, Doris, begged me not to go, of course. The girl’s quite lost her senses since that awful business in the churchyard last night. She’s convinced there’s a maniac about and that any of us could be knocked down at any moment. Poor girl. This whole affair is doing nothing for her nerves, and she was a skittish creature to begin with.”

It piqued Felicity’s interest that Mrs Winterpole also dismissed the lunatic murderer theory. “You don’t feel there’s anything to be afraid of, Mrs Winterpole?”

The older woman’s eyes crinkled sympathetically. “My dear, I know there’s a murderer on the loose, but why would he want to do away with me? Or my nervous maid? We’ve no enemies, and if it was a question of theft, they could steal from us without hanging for it. I tried telling Doris that, of course, but she’s hardly listening to me today. Got a fly under her bonnet about Nora Andrews as well.”

Felicity blinked. “Mr Reeves’ maid?”

“Doris came to me to say she was in a quandary about what to do. I’d never seen the girl so serious.” Mrs Winterpole lowered her voice to a whisper, even though she and Felicity were alone in the lane. “She said she knows Nora to be a liar, and she's wondering if she ought to tell the police."

The hairs on the back of Felicity's neck stood up. "Really," she said, sounding interested but not overly so. "And what makes Nora a liar, according to your maid?"

"Well," began Mrs Winterpole. "On her evenings off, Nora had been telling people she was meeting with her uncle, who's a gamekeeper for Lord Northcote. Only my Doris saw her out with the other gamekeeper. The young one. Oh, I forget his name. Doris said she saw them together more than once. And now she's asking me if she ought to tell the police."

Felicity remembered Mayhew's hawkish face and the sound of the metal file in the gamekeepers' shed. Had it been this liaison, between Nora and Mayhew, that Mr Reeves had objected to when speaking to Lord Northcote? And had Mr Reeves actually had good reason to object? "What did you advise your maid?"

Mrs Winterpole shook her head. "I told Doris to do as she pleases, as it won't make any difference to the outcome of the investigation. Little Nora wouldn't hurt a fly, let alone shoot her employer dead in the middle of the village. Why, I doubt the girl even knows how to pick up a gun, let alone fire one. If she was lying about her friendship with the young gamekeeper, then I don't see what that has to do with the murder. Indeed, I put the question to Doris: if Doris herself were to have a male acquaintance, would it be something she would want to announce to the entire village? I'm sure it wouldn't interest the police in the slightest. Oh, I do despair about that maid of mine. I really do."

Felicity nodded as though in agreement with Mrs Winterpole. Initially, Felicity hadn't imagined Nora capable of being involved in her employer's murder, but had Mr Reeves stayed alive long enough, would the next letter in the mud have been an O?

"In any case," continued Mrs Winterpole. "Whether or not there's someone hiding in the bushes waiting to do away with me, I must get along. I've an appointment for bridge with the Broughtons after dinner, and I simply can't be late for it. I wish you a pleasant walk, Lady Felicity."

With Mrs Winterpole proceeding up the lane behind her, Felicity walked on towards Lower Diddleton, quickening her pace. Despite the older woman's relaxed attitude, something about the conversation with Mrs Winterpole had unnerved Felicity. She needed to speak to Alex. Their plans would have to change.

Chapter Twenty-Five

Keeping to the lanes away from the high street and village green, Felicity moved quickly towards the Cat and Cream, its large thatched roof visible above the smaller shops and cottages surrounding it. Lower Diddleton had already been buzzing with police after Mr Reeves' murder, but following the shooting of Mr McNabb just the night before, the village was now full to bursting with dark blue uniforms and detectives in overcoats. On her way towards the inn, Felicity passed a pair of police officers patrolling the village's back lanes. They touched their hats to her, and she smiled politely in return. If whoever shot Mr Reeves and Mr McNabb was still in the village, then he — or she — had nerves tougher than steel.

Felicity had decided she would go to the back of the inn, enter through one of the service doors, and somehow find Alex's room. She at least knew it had a view of the green. At the back of the inn was the line of tightly parked motor cars with shining coachwork in black, dark blue, and burgundy. The door to the Cat and Cream's busy kitchen was open, and the smell of that evening's supper — lamb with mint sauce — made Felicity's nose twitch. The back door leading to the reception was closed, but a door to the dining room had been left open. Exactly how she would find Alex's room once inside the inn was a problem Felicity would worry about when she came to it. The first challenge was to get inside without being seen.

She approached the dining room door. Above the clatter of pots and the hissing of pans, shouts could be heard from the kitchen, mostly the head chef giving orders, but it was the approach of familiar voices that prompted Felicity to dive behind one of the motors.

"No, Father. I had no such problems with the man." The nasally tone was that of the inn's landlord, Mr Chesterton. "And I'm very happy to be able to say that. Sounds as if he was a nasty piece of work."

"I suppose that's one way of putting it, but it's not always clear why people do what they do," came the response.

Felicity slid her white picture hat from her head and inched her nose above the door of the Morris Oxford beside which she was crouched. Her suspicions were confirmed: Father Neil was with Mr Chesterton. They were exiting the inn via the open kitchen door.

As Felicity sank behind the Morris and pulled on her hat, the vicar continued to address the landlord. "I'm certainly glad you had no bother from the man. I've checked with just about every business owner in the parish, and it seems he'd approached no one locally."

"Glad to hear it," came Mr Chesterton's reply. To Felicity's relief, it sounded as though the two men had stopped close to the kitchen door. Her hiding place was safe for now. "Running a business is enough of a burden as it is. I've a busy life and no Mrs Chesterton to turn to for comfort at the end of a demanding day." It was the first time Felicity had heard Mr Chesterton present himself as at all vulnerable. He'd always struck her as the mercenary sort.

"I can only imagine," replied Father Neil, full of sympathy. "To think that Mr Reeves was a blackmailer. Who could have known that such an objectionable character walked among us, here in Lower Diddleton?"

So it was now common knowledge that Mr Reeves had been a blackmailer. Felicity continued to listen.

"Had I known," continued the vicar, "I might have framed things rather differently at his memorial service."

"Or not given him one at all," suggested the landlord.

"Oh, I don't think I'd have gone that far. He'd not been convicted of it."

"True, true. And I must say, the reception after the memorial service was quite the money spinner. A death in the parish seems to put people in the mood for a cherry slice or two."

After an awkward silence followed by a brusque farewell, Mr Chesterton re-entered the inn's kitchen and began issuing orders to his staff, while the vicar started moving in Felicity's direction, his footsteps tapping along the paving at the back of the inn.

How would she explain herself if Father Neil caught her crouching behind the Morris?

On her hands and knees, Felicity crawled out from between the motors and, still stooped low behind some conveniently placed hedging, hurried along the lane and away from the inn. At a safe distance, Felicity stood up straight, shook the dirt off her skirt, and trotted along a little, putting some extra distance between herself and the vicar. She then dropped into a casual walking rhythm as though out for a stroll in the direction of the village high street.

"Lady Felicity?" The vicar called out to her. "Is that you?"

Turning, Felicity feigned surprise and gave the vicar a sunny smile. "Father Neil," she said, pleasantly surprised by her own composure and acting abilities. "Whatever are you doing here?"

The breeze caught Father Neil's wispy grey hair and made it dance, but his face was serious. "I hope there are no hard feelings between us, Lady Felicity."

"Why ever should there be?" said Felicity before realising what the vicar was referring to. Their disagreement over the parish newsletter had happened only the day before. "Oh, of course not. Water under the bridge. Consider it all forgotten." She gave him another sunny smile.

"Glad to hear it." The vicar smiled serenely back at her. "Very glad to hear it."

While Felicity's mission to contact Alex had been more than a little derailed, there was another opportunity to gather information for the story she and Alex were working on. "Father, may I ask you something?"

"Of course, my lady."

"Is it true that Mr Reeves was—" Felicity lowered her voice to a whisper. "—a blackmailer?"

Father Neil's brow crumpled. "Yes, my lady. I'm afraid it's true. You or any of your family weren't — how can I say — affected at all, were you?"

"Oh, no. Not at all. Thankfully." Felicity lowered her voice again. "But was he blackmailing anyone here, in the parish?"

The vicar sighed. "When I heard from the police that they'd discovered Mr Reeves to be involved in blackmail, I made it my business to check on the parishioners. My impression is that Mr Reeves wasn't carrying out his disgraceful deeds locally, so I suppose we can at least be grateful for that."

Felicity nodded thoughtfully. "So if revenge for blackmail was the motive," she murmured, "it must have been someone from outside Lower Diddleton."

"I'm sorry, my lady. What did you say?"

Felicity looked up at the vicar. He wasn't the right person to discuss her theories with. "Oh, nothing. Just, you know, talking to myself." She gave the vicar another winsome smile. "As one does, sometimes."

The vicar smiled back. "I quite understand, my lady. I quite often do it myself."

"Well," said Felicity, her mind returning to the problem of how to contact Alex. "Please don't let me hold you up any longer, Father Neil. I'm certain there are many more members of our parish who could benefit from your reassurance and wisdom at this difficult time."

"Actually, Lady Felicity," said the vicar a little awkwardly. "I was wondering if I might ask you something. I was planning to talk to you about it at a later stage, but now seems as opportune a moment as any."

"Please," said Felicity, her curiosity piqued. "Ask away."

"The last time we spoke," said the vicar, "you handed in your notice as editor of the parish newsletter."

Felicity kept her head held high as she nodded. "That's right. I did."

"I was wondering if you'd had any second thoughts about your decision."

Felicity blinked. "Why would I have had second thoughts?"

"It's just..." The vicar became sheepish. "Several parishioners have asked me about the special edition. It seems the local people were looking forward to it, and more specifically, to your insight on the matter of the murder, Lady Felicity."

Felicity's mouth opened and closed in a manner Lady Henrietta would have said reminded her of a goldfish. "Really?"

Father Neil nodded tightly. "I perhaps underestimated how much your writings mean to Lower Diddleton and the surrounding area." He cleared his throat. "I wouldn't want to be the reason the newsletter lost the best writer and editor it had ever known."

Warmth rose in Felicity's chest. "That means a tremendous amount to me. Really, Father Neil, it does."

The vicar smiled. "So you'll come back?"

Felicity looked up at the windows of the inn. In his room, Alex was writing up coverage of the murder that would be read not just by the inhabitants of Lower Diddleton, but by the inhabitants of Sweetbrooke, Exeter, and beyond. Felicity had information she knew Alex would want to hear, both about Nora and the young gamekeeper, Mayhew, and now about Mr Reeves' blackmailing activities in the village, or rather, the lack thereof. She didn't know how the pieces of the puzzle fit together, but she knew that if she could get to Alex, they'd be able to make sense of it together, and the story in the Western Daily News would be stronger for it.

Felicity returned her gaze to the vicar. "I very much appreciate what you've told me, Father Neil. Really, I do. But can I please have some time to think about it? There's something else I must do first."

Chapter Twenty-Six

Having said farewell to the vicar and abandoned all hope of accessing Alex's room via the back or any other entrance at the inn, Felicity already had a new plan. It was so straightforward that she chastised herself for not having come up with it sooner.

Joining the village high street, she walked briskly past the row of pastel-coloured shops. In the grounds of All Angels church, several policemen were still present, examining the grass around the headstones with white-gloved hands and poring over the gravel path for any potentially missed clue. Felicity waited for a greengrocer's van to pass before crossing the road and arriving on the village green. At the far end of the green stood the recently installed, brilliant-white public telephone box. It was coin-operated, and while Felicity had never used it before, she had a small amount of money in her tooled-leather bag as she always did, just in case.

Careful to avoid the muddy gouges made by tyres, Felicity crossed the grass and approached the telephone box, which, thanks to multiple sparkling panes of glass in its walls, was clearly empty.

She pulled open the door and stepped inside.

A list of instructions posted on the wall informed her where to insert her money and how to use buttons A and B. Lifting the earpiece, Felicity put a penny in the coin slot. Standing on tiptoes to speak into the mouthpiece, as it was fixed to the wooden backboard and not attached to a stick like the telephone at Bradley Court, she asked the operator to connect her to the Cat and Cream, then she waited.

"Cat and Cream Inn, Lower Diddleton." The clerk at the end of the line spoke quickly. It didn't sound like the young man Felicity had talked to at the reception desk the day before. "How may I help?"

"Good day. I'd like to send a message to one of your guests, please. Without delay. It's rather urgent."

"Very well." There was the rustling of paper. "We can take it to the room right away. Who shall I say the message is from?"

Felicity had already anticipated this question. "Miss Fenella Quinn."

"Who is your message for, Miss Quinn?"

"Mr Alexander Cooper."

"And the content of your message, please?"

She'd considered this already, as well. "Urgent meeting needed. Change of plan required. Meet me at the orchard on the way to Oakridge Head."

The clerk coughed a little uncomfortably. He perhaps assumed it to be a message related to a romantic liaison, but Felicity wasn't embarrassed in the slightest. It was an exceptional situation demanding extraordinary measures.

"Thank you, Miss Quinn. I've noted it all down. I'll be certain to pass your message onto Mr Cooper just as soon as he returns to the inn."

"As soon as he returns?" The news came as a surprise. "He's not in his room?"

"No, miss. He left the inn a short while ago."

Her brow creased with concern, Felicity thanked the clerk and replaced the receiver.

Hadn't they agreed Alex would work on his article while Felicity went to gather more information? Were they working together on the story or not? She'd trusted Alex and taken him at his word. Had she been wrong about doing so?

She shook her head in an attempt to dislodge the worrisome thoughts from her mind. There was no use in wasting time second-guessing herself. Alex had probably just stepped away from his typewriter to buy a bun from the bakery. It was dinnertime, after all. But as Felicity turned and pushed open the door of the telephone box, she got a rather unpleasant surprise.

With his broad shoulders hunched forward and his hands in his pockets, Alex was waiting outside the telephone box, and he wasn't alone. Beside him stood Jasper, who didn't look pleased at all.

———

As the door of the telephone box fell closed behind her with a soft whoosh, Felicity's stomach sank with dread. The game was up.

Jasper scowled at his sister. "Felicity," he said in his most serious voice, his avoidance of her nickname never a sign of anything good.

Alex wouldn't look at Felicity, but she didn't need to read it in his eyes. He'd betrayed her to her brother. But why? Alex stood to lose from Jasper knowing they'd been working together.

"I don't suppose I need to tell you how thoroughly disappointed I am," said Jasper sternly, his hands pressed into the pockets of the waistcoat of his navy three-piece suit. "I thought we had an understanding."

Felicity took a deep breath and lifted her chin. "I understand you perfectly, Jasper. I'm your little sister, and you want to take care of me."

"It's not about what I want," he replied. "It's about duty. It's my *duty* to take care of you, and if you understand my position, as you claim you do, then why won't you let me do my duty?"

Felicity fired a glance at Alex, but he still wouldn't look at her. She returned her attention to Jasper. "You wanted me to shadow one of your reporters. That's what I've been doing."

"Not on a bally murder case, Felicity," blurted Jasper. "That's not the starting point I wanted for you at all," he said with more control. "I'll not have you follow Coop to the courts."

"The courts?" Felicity looked from Jasper to Alex.

Reluctantly, Alex met her eye. "Lord Northcote will appear before the magistrate in Exeter this afternoon."

Felicity's heart bounced into her throat. "He's being accused of murder?"

"No, Felicity," said Jasper gravely. "He'll be charged under the Firearms Act, for his failure to lock up his weapons."

Felicity's mouth felt dry. "But isn't he a suspect? Isn't this a step towards accusing him of murder?"

"Not necessarily—" began Jasper.

"I want to go," said Felicity abruptly, no longer caring how impudent she sounded. What did she have to lose? "I want to report from the magistrate's court. I want to be there for Uncle Basil."

"Cici," said Jasper imploringly. "Go back to Bradley Court. The Rolls is waiting for you. Let's talk this through when I get home. I've got a matter or two to see to here in the village, but I'm sure we'll sort things out between us when I get home. Please."

Alex's gaze was fixed on the ground. Anger at his betrayal bubbled up inside Felicity, but people passing the village green could already see that there was a rather animated discussion underway between two of the Quick siblings.

"Very well," said Felicity, who had no intention of bringing her family's name into disrepute.

Holding her head high, she walked past Jasper and Alex towards the Rolls, its dark blue coachwork glittering in the sunshine at the side of the green. Upon her approach, Finnegan alighted from the vehicle and held the door open for her, his face as inscrutable as ever despite the Quick family drama beside the telephone box. "Good afternoon, Lady Felicity," he said with a touch of his cap.

"Good afternoon, Finnegan," said Felicity with a tight smile. Her heart was still pumping hard with indignation at Alex's betrayal and Jasper's unwillingness to treat her as a fully fledged adult. None of it was the driver's fault, of course, yet she couldn't quite be her usual gracious self.

As Finnegan returned to his seat behind the steering wheel, and the Rolls' engine purred, Felicity cast a glance around the village, at the church, shops, and cottages. Among the villagers trying to get on with their lives as normally as possible, it was easy to spot the policemen, journalists, and other out-of-towners who had descended on Lower Diddleton. It had once been the sort of village where the most exciting occurrences were the annual maypole dance and the odd Catherine wheel on Bonfire Night. How long would it be before the mysteries of Mr Reeves' death and the shooting of Mr McNabb were solved? How long would it take for village life to get back to normal? Would life ever even go back to normal?

And if the murderer turned out to be a local person — if it turned out to be Lord Northcote — what would that do to the fabric of the community? Worst of all, Felicity was powerless to do anything about it. Indeed, it'd perhaps been an illusion that she'd been anything but powerless since the beginning of the whole sorry affair.

On the other side of the village green, beyond the cluster of trees beside the duck pond, a flurry of activity caught Felicity's eye. Pulled up beside the bright yellow front gate of Mr Reeves' cottage was a dark red motor taxi, the sort that often loitered outside the railway station at Sweetbrooke. Its rotund, flat-capped driver was busy loading several small travelling bags into the vehicle, although bending at the waist was something of a challenge for him. In the back seat sat Nora Andrews, her eyes shifting nervously across the green.

The Rolls pulled away and glided slowly along the village high street as Nora's driver took his seat behind the wheel of the dark red taxi.

"Where are we going, Finnegan?" asked Felicity.

"I understand from Lord Quick that I'm to take you to Bradley Court, my lady."

The taxi pulled away from the gate of Mr Reeves' cottage.

"And what if I told you, Finnegan, that I don't wish to go to Bradley Court?"

Finnegan paused at a junction, his gloved hands resting on the Rolls' steering wheel. "Well, my lady. I'm not under instruction to disobey any order you might wish to give me. So I suppose I would ask you where you would like to go."

The dark red taxi took the turning for the lane towards Sweetbrooke.

"What if I told you," Felicity said, nodding towards the other side of the village green, "that I wanted to follow that taxi?"

Finnegan's hands tightened on the wheel. "I would do as your ladyship instructed."

"Wonderful," said Felicity with a curt nod. "Then, please, let's follow that taxi."

Chapter Twenty-Seven

The Rolls crawled up the narrow, winding lane towards Sweetbrooke, Nora's blue hat and slender shoulders clearly visible in the taxi ahead. She didn't turn around, but even if she had done, would Nora have considered the motor behind her suspicious? Felicity still couldn't quite picture Mr Reeves' former maid as the murderer, but the possibility couldn't be ruled out. As yet, Felicity had no plan for what to do if she caught up with Nora's taxi, but she certainly wouldn't do something silly or dangerous. If she discovered anything incriminating, she'd take it directly to the police.

Felicity was about to pull her notebook out of her pocket to help her get her thoughts straight about what she might say to Nora, but the process was interrupted.

"Looks like they're stopping at Sweetbrooke railway station, my lady," said Finnegan. "Shall I draw up behind the taxi?"

"No, better not," said Felicity, her mind working quickly to balance her desire to speak with the murdered man's maid and the need to avoid any unnecessary risks with her own safety. "You can stop a little further along the lane and wait for me there."

The motor stopped as per her instruction, and Finnegan turned.

His face was as impassive as always with perhaps just a hint of concern at the corners of his eyes. "Will you be taking the train, my lady?"

"That's not my intention, Finnegan. I hope to return to you before not too long."

Upon alighting from the Rolls, Felicity walked quickly back along the lane shaded by rows of beech towards the station, the leaves of the trees gently hissing in the late afternoon breeze.

With its iron- and woodwork painted glossy green with accents of red and gold, Sweetbrooke station was picturesque. Even the stationmaster's cottage at the front, built in pinkish sandstone, its window boxes stuffed with white geraniums and trailing ivy, was pretty enough to feature on the top of a chocolate box. Although Sweetbrooke was only slightly larger than Lower Diddleton, its station served several local parishes and brought many tourists to and from the area.

Felicity couldn't spot Nora or the rotund, flat-capped taxi driver among the bustle of people and vehicles at the front of the station. A blackboard announced that the next departure would be a service to Exeter, from where there were connections onward to London or the North of England. Felicity lifted onto tiptoes as she joined the flow of people entering the station, trying to spot Nora's blue hat and narrow shoulders. Crossing the cast-iron footbridge, Felicity descended onto the platform for Exeter, which was already busy with passengers awaiting the next train. There were mothers with children holding their hands, perhaps heading home after visiting relatives in the countryside, and smiling young couples who'd maybe been to one of the local villages for a cream tea and a ride in a horse and cart. The stationmaster stood on the edge of the platform in his neatly pressed uniform, a whistle around his neck and a flag in his hand, checking his wristwatch.

As Felicity made her way past the waiting passengers and porters on-hand to help them, she spotted Nora. She was standing at the very end of the platform and glanced nervously around her, both in the direction from which the train was to arrive and towards the footbridge at the other end of the platform. Two tired-looking leather valises sat on the ground next to her, and she had a satchel-style bag over her shoulder, the strap of which she gripped tightly with both hands. Nora looked nothing like a killer. She looked like a lost little girl on the verge of tears.

Surrounded by so many people, including the station's staff, Felicity considered the risk of Nora pointing a gun at her to be minimal. Still, she approached the young maid slowly. Nora didn't recognise Felicity until she was almost upon her, and the girl's brown eyes widened with surprise.

"L-Lady Felicity."

"Nora," said Felicity with a kind smile. "Fancy seeing you here. Where are you headed?"

Nora swallowed, her nervous gaze jumping between Felicity and the steadily filling platform. "I'm going home, my lady. I'm going back to stay with family in Taunton until I can find another position."

"Oh, you're returning to Somerset. Was there no position for you locally?"

Nora gave a decisive shake of her head. "I'd rather go home, my lady. I'd rather not stay here."

"Quite so," said Felicity gently. "There's nothing like being among one's own people. And I can't imagine you have very fond memories of Lower Diddleton after all that's happened here."

Nora said nothing. She turned to look along the track, which disappeared around a grassy hill. The train for Exeter was due any moment. Felicity had no time to waste.

"There's something I've been very keen to ask your opinion on, Nora," she said. "Would you mind awfully if I put a question to you?"

Nora blinked at Felicity. "What's that, my lady?"

"I don't suppose you know," began Felicity, "but Lord Northcote was a very good friend of my late father's. I'm therefore quite surprised by the police's interest in him. You see, I know Lord Northcote, and I know he would never murder a man. I wanted to ask you, Nora, seeing as you knew your employer probably better than anyone in the area. Who do you think killed Mr Reeves?"

The colour drained from Nora's cheeks. "I told the police already." Her voice wobbled. "I know nothing about it, my lady."

"Perhaps you don't know for certain," said Felicity carefully. "But you surely must have ideas of your own about the matter. Do you not have an opinion on the subject?"

"Really, my lady. I don't know anything about it. I didn't see or hear anything, and I already told the police as much. I didn't know it was going to happen. How could I?" Nora bit her lip as she looked towards bridge between the platforms, her brown eyes wide with worry.

"Are you waiting for someone?" Felicity asked.

"What?" said Nora abruptly. "Sorry, my lady. No. I'm not waiting for anyone."

A puff of steam appeared from behind the hill.

"And what do you suppose the letter N might mean?" said Felicity, perhaps a little too boldly, but time was running out.

"The letter N?" Nora went paler still. "W-what's the letter N got to do with anything?"

Felicity's heart beat hard in her chest. "Mr Reeves wrote a letter N in the mud where he died."

"Did he?" Nora's brow creased. "An N? H-how do you know?"

Felicity said nothing for a moment, merely raising her eyebrows at the maid. "I saw it myself. What do you suppose it stands for?"

"N as in..." Nora shook her head. "Oh, no, my lady. No. You don't think... You don't think I had a hand in Mr Reeves' death, do you?"

"I don't know, Nora," said Felicity carefully. "Did you?"

Nora shook her head hard, screwing up her eyes as though willing the world to disappear. "I told you already. I wasn't involved. I couldn't have known what would happen. Really, I couldn't. I just want to go home. I want to be left alone. Why won't people leave me alone?"

As the train neared the station, Nora leaned forward to pick up her valises. It was clear she wasn't telling Felicity everything she knew, but what could Felicity do? She couldn't force a confession from the girl.

The train blew its whistle upon entering the station, its wheels and cranks slowing and its black-painted boiler shining in the evening sun. As the passenger carriages rolled by, Nora stepped away from Felicity and towards the edge of the platform. "Sorry to not be more help, my lady," she said, sounding more relieved than apologetic. "The third-class carriages stop here. I imagine you'll be wanting to travel in first."

Nora looked back at Felicity with a meek but satisfied smile, then something further up the platform beyond Felicity caught Nora's attention, and her smile faltered. Her cheeks went ashen.

Felicity turned.

Mayhew, the younger of Lord Northcote's gamekeepers, was coming towards them, and the look on his face was of barely concealed rage.

Chapter Twenty-Eight

Passengers either stepped aside or were pushed as Mayhew made his way towards Felicity and Nora. He was of average height and slight of frame, but there was strength to his wiriness, and his eyes were focused on Nora like a hawk fixed on its prey.

"No," Nora whispered, her lower lip trembling as the carriages of the train slowed to a stop alongside the platform.

"Mr Mayhew—" began Felicity, but he jostled her aside as if he hadn't seen her.

Approaching Nora, Mayhew grabbed the maid's wrist with a large-knuckled hand.

"Where do you think you're going?" he growled, his jaw taut with agitation.

Nora shrank back from him. "I want to go home. I didn't tell anyone. I'll never tell anyone. Please, I just want to go home."

The doors of the carriages opened, and the platform was suddenly abuzz with movement as passengers alighted from and joined the train, with luggage hoisted in both directions.

Mayhew yanked on Nora's arm, and she squealed, but her cry went unnoticed by anyone other than Felicity on the busy platform.

"I waited for you," he said, his eyes wild with anger. "Put my neck on the line for you, I did. And now you're running away? You said you'd come with me."

"That was before I knew what you done," Nora sobbed. "But I never told anyone. I never will." A tear rolled down her cheek. "Please, Paul. You're hurting me."

Felicity stepped forward. She didn't know what to do, but she couldn't stand by and do nothing.

"Mr Mayhew," she said, more firmly this time.

"What?" Mayhew span towards Felicity as though noticing her for the first time. "Wait. I know you." His gaze switched between Felicity and Nora. "In this together, are you? Helping her get away from me, is that what's going on? I suppose Nora's told you all about me, has she? I suppose she's told you everything." He pulled again on Nora's arm, eliciting a yelp from the terrified girl. "Nasty little minx. You had me fooled, you did. I'll not let you get away with it."

"That's just it, Mr Mayhew," said Felicity, her voice calm and firm, as though addressing a naughty dog. "Nora hasn't even mentioned your name. We bumped into one another here, at the station, and the only thing she's told me is that she's travelling to stay with family in Somerset."

Tears rolled down Nora's cheeks. "It's true, Paul. I've said nothing about you."

The activity on the platform was easing. The newly arrived passengers were making their way over the bridge, and the porters were closing the carriage doors. One of them called out to Nora, who still had her bags in her hands. "Will you be boarding, miss?"

Mayhew's lip quivered into a sneer. By preventing Nora from boarding the train, he'd drawn attention to himself. Might he do something desperate?

"Please, Paul," said Nora beseechingly. "I did everything you wanted. Please believe me. Please let me go."

Mayhew's expression darkened. "Can't very well do that, now, can I?" He reached into the pocket of his jacket. "I'm sure her ladyship has heard enough." There was a metallic snap, like the hammer on a revolver being pulled back. Though concealed in his pocket, the shape of the gun's muzzle was clear enough through the fabric of Mayhew's jacket as he levelled the weapon first at Nora and then at Felicity. "Get on the train," he said.

Felicity's stomach plummeted.

The stationmaster blew his whistle. "Last chance to board," he called.

"Get in," said Mayhew through gritted teeth. "Both of you."

As Nora began weeping, all Felicity could think about was how disappointed Jasper would be. Allowing herself to be kidnapped by a murderer really took the biscuit in terms of getting into dangerous situations. But when Felicity looked along the platform, her heart surged. There was hope, and she knew exactly what she had to do.

Mayhew jerked Nora's arm. "Don't make a scene," he said. "I'm warning you. Just get on the blasted train." As he let go of Nora's wrist, he flung her towards the door of a nearby carriage.

Her head bowed and shoulders shaking, Nora began lifting her bags on board.

"And you," said Mayhew, aiming the pocketed gun at Felicity. "Get on the train."

Felicity didn't move. "Where are you taking us?"

"Doesn't matter, does it? Just do as I say."

"But what will you do with us?"

"I'll figure that out later." Mayhew took a step towards Felicity, jabbing the concealed gun towards her. "Just do what I tell you."

Felicity folded her arms over her chest. Her heart was pounding harder than it ever had. "And what if I refuse to go with you?"

Mayhew's eyes quivered with rage. "Oh. You'll go with me, all right."

"She won't."

Alex's voice surprised Mayhew and caused him to turn away from Felicity. Alex brought his arm down like an axe, pushing Mayhew's hand and the pocketed gun towards the ground. Felicity stepped backwards, drawing a hand to her chest as Alex began grappling with Mayhew. Nora turned and screamed, prompting the stationmaster to blow his whistle as he came running along the platform. A second whistle blew. Coming down off the footbridge were two police officers in uniform, one running much faster than the other.

Mayhew would be overpowered. There was no chance for him to escape. He had played a dangerous game and lost.

Then the gun went off with a deafening bang.

Chapter Twenty-Nine

Sweetbrooke station wasn't big enough for a waiting room or refreshments counter, so the stationmaster offered his cottage for the police's use. With its low ceiling and floral theme, the cottage's sitting room was cosy, if a little cramped. The stationmaster's wife, with her round, friendly face and a green striped apron tied at her waist, bustled quietly between the sitting room and kitchen with warm drinks, slices of ginger cake, and fresh cheese straws.

Beside the fireplace, Felicity sat on the edge of a wingback chair upholstered in a pale lemon chintz. She was holding a china cup full of hot, milky tea that trembled a little in its saucer. She rarely took her tea with sugar, but the stationmaster's wife had insisted it would do Felicity the world of good, and she hadn't been wrong.

Having finished her account of matters to the police, Felicity's nerves were at last settling. Other than being somewhat overwhelmed at everything that had happened, she was, thankfully, completely unharmed.

"And how did you know the suspect would come to..." Chief Inspector Luscombe glanced at his notepad. "Sweetbrooke station?"

The chief inspector had arrived in one of several police cars that had raced up from Lower Diddleton, bells ringing, shortly after Paul

Mayhew and Nora Andrews had been apprehended. In his long grey overcoat, his trilby resting on the low table at the centre of the little sitting room, Chief Inspector Luscombe stood just inside the doorway with only an inch between his balding head and the ceiling.

"We didn't, sir," said Sergeant Hodgkins, who stood rather proudly next to an oak dresser filled with plates. Beside him stood Constable Price, his helmet under his arm and his head stooped to avoid dabbing brilliantine on the sitting room's ceiling.

Despite her earlier misgivings about the two local policemen, Felicity had been extremely grateful when they'd arrived at Sweetbrooke station to arrest Mayhew. The N in the mud they'd accidentally destroyed had proved rather misleading. Felicity realised now that it likely hadn't been an N at all, but an unfinished M.

Sergeant Hodgkins glanced at Alex. "We were alerted to a potential situation by Mr Cooper here."

On the opposite side of the fireplace, Alex was sitting on a chair identical to the one Felicity was perched upon, with his jacket hung over the chair's back. He was in a grey waistcoat and white shirt, with a sleeve rolled up to reveal a neatly applied bandage on his right forearm.

When Mayhew's gun went off, the bullet grazed Alex's arm but miraculously did no further damage, neither to Alex nor to anyone else.

He lifted his teacup to his lips and sipped from it calmly. Alex's eyes met Felicity's, and she smiled. Whatever had led to Alex telling Jasper about their collaboration could be forgotten. Felicity would be forever indebted to him for arriving on the platform just in time.

The sergeant continued. "Our duties were done for the day in Lower Diddleton. We were returning to Sweetbrooke when Mr Cooper asked if he might ride with us in the Ford, as he was keen to follow Lady Felicity and her driver. He said he'd just seen her ladyship depart for Sweetbrooke."

The chief inspector raised his eyebrows as he turned to Alex. "What gave you concern for Lady Felicity's welfare, Mr Cooper?"

Alex returned his teacup to its saucer. "After Lady Felicity's motor departed, I saw the gamekeeper Mayhew run across the village green, jump into a vehicle, and set off after her."

"Where had Mayhew come from?"

"That I didn't see. Perhaps from Reeves' cottage. Certainly from that direction."

"And what vehicle was he driving?" asked the chief inspector, making notes as he spoke.

"A van," said Alex. "Green and black. Looked like something the gamekeepers might use around the estate. Mayhew jumped in and tore off up the lane behind the Rolls-Royce. The lad seemed frightfully worked up. I hadn't seen Nora Andrews leave the village in the taxi, so my assumption was that Mayhew was following Lady Felicity." Alex glanced at her, his blue eyes flashing. "I didn't like the look of it at all. So I approached Sergeant Hodgkins and Constable Price, just as the sergeant said."

"What happened next?" asked the chief inspector, switching his gaze between Alex and the sergeant.

"We came across the vehicles, sir," said Sergeant Hodgkins, "not far from Sweetbrooke station."

"It crossed my mind that Mayhew was perhaps late for a train," added Alex, "and that Lady Felicity had been on her way to somewhere else, but I wanted to be certain. So I went into the station. As soon as I got onto the footbridge, I spotted Lady Felicity with Mayhew. I must admit, I rather raced onto the platform without thinking. When I tackled Mayhew, I hadn't really thought the whole thing through. The gun going off rather brought me to my senses." Alex looked at his bandage sheepishly. "I suppose you'll tell me I acted like a ruddy fool."

Chief Inspector Luscombe paused his note-taking. "You were in the war, I take it, Mr Cooper?"

Alex nodded. "Fifth Battalion, London Rifles."

"Do you think the Fifth Battalion would have got very far if you'd all just sat around waiting for someone else to make the first move?"

Alex huffed and smiled. "I see your point."

"And I can't ignore, Mr Cooper, that it's mainly thanks to you we'll have our murderer before the magistrate in the morning."

"Has he confessed?" asked Felicity, setting her empty teacup and its saucer on the side table at her elbow. "It's rather obvious it was him, from everything he said to Nora, but he didn't exactly say that he'd pulled the trigger on either Mr Reeves or Mr McNabb."

Chief Inspector Luscombe shook his head. "My men tell me Mayhew's giving us the silent treatment. He's going to be a hard nut to crack. Miss Andrews, on the other hand, is helping us along very nicely."

Felicity raised her eyebrows. "I suppose it's safe for her to share what she knows with Mayhew in custody. He behaved in a rather beastly manner towards her. She was terrified of him."

"Miss Andrews certainly lied to us before," said the chief inspector. "Claimed she didn't really know Mayhew, but she's taken that all back now, of course."

Reaching around, Alex took his notebook from his jacket's inside pocket. He turned to Chief Inspector Luscombe. "Can I ask a few questions on behalf of the Western Daily News?"

Felicity smiled. Wounded or not, it was indeed hard to let go of a story once one had one's teeth into it.

Chief Inspector Luscombe sighed. "If it were any other member of the press, the answer would be no. But since it's you, Mr Cooper, I suppose we can make an exception."

"Do we know why Mayhew did it?" asked Alex.

"So far we only have what Miss Andrews has told us, but it seems to have been a case of revenge."

"Revenge for what?" asked Alex.

"Might I hazard a guess?" enquired Felicity. "I've been pondering the matter."

The chief inspector lifted an eyebrow. "Please, my lady."

"Well, we know that Mr Reeves was a blackmailer," began Felicity. "But he wasn't a blackmailer of servants, as they're not the sort to have money. And we also know he wasn't blackmailing anyone locally. So was Mayhew seeking revenge on behalf of someone else?

Perhaps a relative? The other gamekeeper mentioned to us that Mayhew was the son of a suicide."

The chief inspector nodded. "That's right. His father. It seems Mayhew's father had been one of Reeves' victims."

"Well done, my lady," said Sergeant Hodgkins as he and Constable Price sat down to receive a tray of refreshments brought through by the stationmaster's wife. "Quite a talent for deduction you seem to have there."

"What did Reeves do to Mayhew's father?" asked Alex.

"His father owned a small chain of shops in the Bristol area before the war. Through his work as an accountant, Reeves learned of some minor irregularities in the book-keeping. Nothing too serious, but enough that if it were to come out, it could damage his reputation locally."

"The sly devil," said Alex. "He must have been on the lookout for precisely such cases."

"At first, Mayhew's father paid Reeves what he asked," continued the chief inspector. "Then it got too much, and it drove Mayhew's father over the edge. Mayhew himself was just a child at the time."

Felicity brought a hand to her chest. "It's not right to have sympathy for a murderer, of course, but what an absolutely frightful beginning to a young man's life."

Chief Inspector Luscombe went on. "Mayhew's mother was left in a precarious situation, with no one to take on the business. She and the boy went from comfort to poverty rather quickly, and it seems Mayhew's mother brought him up to know the story of her husband's demise. His mother died from illness when Mayhew was just fourteen. After that, the young Mayhew made it his life's work to find Reeves and get revenge for what he did to his family."

Alex shook his head as he continued to write in his notebook. "He certainly opened up to young Nora, didn't he? What's her role in all of this?"

The chief inspector's brow furrowed. "If we take her story at face value, then Andrews says they met in the village after Mayhew started work on the Northcote estate last year. She took pity on him, apparently. He told her his story, about everything that had happened to his father and mother, but Nora hadn't fully understood that her employer was the intended target of Mayhew's revenge. She also claims not to have known that Mayhew's plan for revenge included murder."

Felicity nodded. "That's precisely how she struck me. A naïve young girl caught up in something beyond her understanding and control."

"Not so naïve that she couldn't lie to the police the first time we interviewed her," said Chief Inspector Luscombe.

"I suppose not," replied Felicity thoughtfully.

"Why was Mayhew chasing Nora?" asked Alex. "To silence her?"

"It's a little more complicated than that," said the chief inspector. "Mayhew wasn't simply using Andrews to get closer to Reeves. Mayhew claimed he was in love with the girl. By killing Reeves, Mayhew wasn't just avenging his father, he was delivering Andrews from an evil man's clutches. At least that's what he told her after the deed had been done."

Alex shook his head. "Well, I'll be dashed."

"Mayhew had planned an escape for them both," continued Chief Inspector Luscombe. "They were to sail from Southampton to begin new lives in South America. Except Andrews tells us she was horrified by the idea. Prior to the murder, he'd proposed that they might one day start a new life abroad together, and she'd been considering it, but after Mayhew told her he'd killed Reeves, she was horrified. He wanted to escape with her immediately after the murder, but Andrews refused. At least, that's her story."

"I imagine we'll know more in the coming days," said Alex as he continued to make notes. "Can I turn to you if I need more information, chief inspector?"

Chief Inspector Luscombe nodded stiffly. "I suppose so."

"I've a question, if I may," said Felicity.

The inspector raised his eyebrows at her.

"Why did Paul Mayhew shoot Mr McNabb?"

"Do we know for certain it was Mayhew that did it?" added Alex.

"At this stage, we can only assume it was him, but I'd say it's a firm assumption. If McNabb was asking questions around the village — and I understand he wasn't the subtlest of investigators — Mayhew likely imagined McNabb was interested in Mayhew's own links to Reeves."

Felicity nodded. "If his original plan was to flee with Nora directly after the murder, watching the police carry out their investigations would have taken its toll on Mayhew's nerves. It was quite a gamble to shoot Mr Reeves in the middle of the village like that."

"Indeed. If Mayhew had his way, he and Andrews would be in the Argentine by now, and the whole sorry affair would have a different ending. The lad will no doubt hang for his crimes. Hard to imagine that's what his father or mother would have wanted." The chief inspector sighed and leaned forward to retrieve his trilby from the table. "Before I go, there's something I must ask you, Lady Felicity. Why did you not bring your suspicions about Nora Andrews directly to the police?"

Felicity glanced at Sergeant Hodgkins and Constable Price. Their concentration was on the hot buttered tea cakes the stationmaster's wife had just brought them. Butter dripped onto Constable Price's uniform as he bit into his half.

Felicity turned a polite smile on the chief inspector. "Next time," she said. "I will consider doing exactly that."

Chapter Thirty

The sun was low in the sky when Felicity stepped out of the stationmaster's cottage at the front of Sweetbrooke railway station. The doorway was framed by a tumble of sweetly scented honeysuckle, and a blackbird at the top of a nearby rowan filled the warm evening air with its sweet, liquid song. If it weren't for the police vehicles filling the area where taxis usually waited, it had all the trappings of a completely normal early summer evening at Sweetbrooke station.

Finnegan had found a spot directly in front of the cottage on the other side of the road. Upon seeing Felicity, he alighted from the Rolls and opened a passenger door with an efficient nod in her direction. It was indeed time to return to Bradley Court. She was looking forward to supper and a long night of restful sleep, uninterrupted by ruminations over the murder mystery on her own doorstep, for it was a mystery no longer. The case had been solved.

"I didn't tell Jasper."

Felicity turned. Alex stood in the cottage's doorway, glancing up at her as he rolled his shirtsleeve down over his bandaged arm.

She shook her head a little. "Didn't tell him what?"

"About us working together," Alex continued, walking slowly towards Felicity. "Someone saw us coming back from visiting

McNabb. Jasper wouldn't tell me who, of course, but I suppose that's a lesson for both of us." Alex pulled on his jacket, wincing as he did so. "We shouldn't underestimate what it takes to fool your brother."

Felicity smiled. "He is a Quick, after all. Not much gets past us." She paused for a moment as the blackbird continued to sing. "And while I'm relieved to hear you're not a traitor, I'd have been willing to forgive you, given everything that's happened."

Alex smiled back at Felicity. "Thanks." Inhaling deeply, he gazed out across the police activity, frustrated taxi drivers, and alarmed and curious railway passengers at the front of the station. "Hard to believe it's really over. It all happened so quickly."

"Is it always like this? Covering a murder story, I mean."

"I've worked on a few in my time, but this is the first in which I've been quite so involved," said Alex with a glance at his injured forearm.

Felicity bit her lip. "Will you be all right?"

Alex nodded confidently. "It's just a scratch."

"I feel somewhat responsible," said Felicity sheepishly. "That you had to become so involved."

"We were working on the story together, weren't we? I couldn't leave a fellow reporter in the lurch."

"I'm extremely thankful you didn't," said Felicity, though she wondered if she'd have been able to do the same for Alex had the situation been reversed. "And I imagine Nora is, too. What will happen to her, do you think? I hate to think she'll be treated the same as Mayhew."

"She won't be, but she won't get off scot-free. Had she been honest with the police from the beginning, things might not have got this far."

Felicity nodded thoughtfully. "Perhaps I'm being overly sensitive to her cause as a fellow female, but I rather suspect it was a stroke of bad luck that Nora got in with Mayhew at all."

Alex raised his eyebrows. "The gun Mayhew had with him on the platform belonged to Reeves, you know. Nora allowed him to take it from the cottage. He used it on McNabb, then on me."

Felicity felt a tinge of colour rise to her cheeks, ashamed of her apparently misplaced sympathy. "Well, I'm certainly glad it's all over, and that you're not more injured than you are."

Alex smiled and shook his head. "I've been through worse. Now, you'll have to excuse me, Felicity, as I've a story to write up and copy to turn in. The Western Daily News will have quite the scoop in the morning."

"Can I help?"

"You've done enough, and I've already written everything down." He tapped his jacket where he kept his notepad in the inside pocket. "Just need to give it some shape and telephone it in. Won't take me long."

A secret wave of relief passed through Felicity. She was feeling quite tired and looking forward to getting home. "Can we run you down to Lower Diddleton?"

The door to the cottage slammed shut behind them. "We shall need to leave now, Mr Cooper, if we're to bring you to Lower Diddleton," said Sergeant Hodgkins, who, accompanied by Constable Price, went striding towards one of the black Model Ts pulled up in front of the station. "Mrs Hodgkins will not be at all pleased if I'm late for my supper."

Alex looked at Felicity. "Thank you, but I already accepted an offer from the sergeant. It's probably best if you get back to Bradley Court and get some rest."

Felicity could only agree. "I'll do exactly that."

As the Model T's engine started up, Alex set off towards the police motor. "And perhaps talk to your brother?" he said over his shoulder. "I'm sure he'll be relieved to know you're unharmed."

"I'm sure he will," she sighed. As glad as Felicity would be to get back to Bradley Court, seeing Jasper was the last thing she wanted to do.

Chapter Thirty-One

When Felicity arrived back at Bradley Court, the sun had already dipped below the treetops that were now silhouettes in a powder-blue sky. As she stepped through the thick oak doors and into the cool quiet of the entrance hall, she felt a mix of relief and trepidation. Her spirits were lifted, however, by the sound of little paws scrabbling over the hall's black-and-white tiles, and Pip came dashing towards her in a rare display of enthusiastic affection.

"Why, hello there," said Felicity, scooping the little dog into her arms as he gave her chin copious licks. "Steady on, old chap. What's got into you?"

"Oh, Felicity. Where have you been?" Lady Henrietta appeared in the doorway to the drawing room, a length of shimmering beads hanging from her high-necked dress. "I heard there was quite a commotion at Sweetbrooke earlier. Shots fired, even. Please, do say you were nowhere near any of it."

"I'm all in one piece, Grandmama," said Felicity slightly evasively as Pip continued to lick her chin.

"And you missed dinner, dear. What did I tell you about looking after yourself? No man wants a bag of bones for a wife, even in this day and age."

"I know, Grandmama." Usually Felicity would challenge Lady Henrietta on such statements, but she had quite some other matters on her mind. She placed Pip on the ground. "Is Jasper home?"

The little dog's ears pricked at the familiar noise of a car drawing up on the gravel outside.

"Well, dear, he had some business to attend to in Lower Diddleton, but I believe that's Jasper in the Bentley just now. Why, dear? Must you speak with your brother?"

"Yes," said Felicity, her stomach suddenly tense. "I believe I must."

Illuminated by the green glass lamp on his desk, Jasper lit a pipe. Behind him, the windows overlooking the garden, now cast in twilight, threw back a reflection of the study's interior. Felicity could see herself seated on the other side of her brother's voluminous desk, her bobbed curls a little dishevelled, Pip sitting alert on her lap. As Jasper, eyebrows lowered, puffed up a cloud of smoke that swirled around him, Felicity said nothing. The less she said, the sooner the telling-off would be over, and the sooner she could go to bed.

Jasper's moustache twitched. "I heard about everything."

Felicity swallowed. "Everything?"

"Everything that happened at Sweetbrooke station today."

Felicity nodded gravely. It was a minor victory that her whereabouts on the night of Mr McNabb's shooting seemed somehow to have remained hers and Alex's secret.

"You can imagine my feelings about the whole bally thing," said Jasper, his words punctuated with puffs of smoke like an angry dragon.

Felicity opened her mouth, then she remembered her plan and closed it again.

"It's typical Coop, flying in to save the day." Jasper shook his head. "Saw him do it many times in the trenches, putting himself at risk. But he wouldn't have needed to today had you not gone running after Reeves' maid."

Felicity pressed her lips together as Pip shifted on her lap. Her plan for silence was harder to carry out than she'd imagined. She was under no illusions about the danger she'd been in at the station, and she wasn't the type to crave accolades, but had Felicity not followed Nora to Sweetbrooke, then perhaps Mayhew never would have been caught at all.

"I'm also not at all keen on how you dragged Finnegan into this whole bally thing," continued Jasper. "I'm sure the poor fellow feels quite terrible about having delivered you into danger like that. Seriously, Felicity. What were you thinking?"

Jasper stared at Felicity, waiting for her reaction. She stared back at him, desperately fighting the urge to reply.

"Do you not give a jot about any of the people that care about you?" he urged. "Do you not care how worried I or Grandmama would have been?"

"Of course I jolly well do, Jasper!" The words burst from Felicity's mouth without her wanting them to. "I'm not a monster. But if I hadn't done it, if I hadn't followed Nora to the station, Mayhew would have got away, and he'd have taken Nora with him. Don't you see?"

It was Jasper's turn to be silent. He sucked on his pipe. "So you were fully aware of the danger you were getting yourself into?"

"If you mean did I know in advance that I would have a gun pointed at me, then no, I had no clue of what I was getting myself into."

Jasper hunkered down in his chair, chewing unhappily on the mouthpiece of his pipe. Felicity drew in a deep breath and scowled, cross at herself for doing a rotten job of keeping quiet.

After much staring and pipe-puffing, Jasper spoke. "I could ask you why you wouldn't leave things alone, especially after the last talk we had. But I already know the answer."

Felicity narrowed her eyes at her brother. "How do you know the answer?" She wasn't sure of it herself.

Jasper narrowed his eyes back at her. "It's obvious. You're a Quick, Felicity. That's all there is to it. You're the first among the women of our family to display the trait, but one can't be too surprised about that sort of thing these days."

"The trait?" asked Felicity, curiosity getting the better of her. "What trait?"

Jasper stood up from his chair and began pacing in front of the window. "The newsman's trait." He glanced at Felicity. "Or the newswoman's trait," he added with a twitch of his moustache.

Felicity stroked Pip's head. "Go on," she said.

"It's the need to know," said Jasper. "The inability to leave things unexplained. You want to know not just what is happening, but *why* it's happening. Once on the scent, there's no stopping you. You have to see it through to the end." Jasper puffed some more on his pipe. "Father was blind to it, of course, but I'd always suspected you had it, Cici, and this whole murder business has illustrated just how deeply it runs in you."

Felicity frowned, confused. This wasn't the telling-off she'd been expecting. "Are you saying I was born to be a news reporter?"

Jasper stopped pacing, removed his pipe from his mouth, and turned towards Felicity, placing his hands on his desk. "Now, look. Just because you have the trait, doesn't mean you have *carte blanche* to report on whatever bally topic takes your fancy. It can be dangerous, and you've seen that now." He stood up straight, his moustache twitching. "But yes. It's clear — to me, at least — that you're a born journalist."

Felicity's stomach did a little flip. She did her best to prevent the corners of her mouth from sliding upward into a grin. "So you support me? With my intentions for my career?"

"Cici, my dearest sister. It might not have always seemed that way to you, but I promise, I've always been prepared to support you."

"Oh, Jasper," said Felicity, clapping her hands together and making Pip jump. "I'm so happy I could hug you."

"Steady on, old girl," said Jasper as he sat back down. "Let's not go over the top, shall we?" He put his pipe in an ashtray and leaned back in his chair. "With both our parents gone, precisely what my role should be in your life is not clear to me. You're a grown woman, after all. But one thing is certain. I'm your elder brother — always have been, always will be — and I care for you very much."

Felicity smiled. Her heart was overflowing with love for Jasper and with relief that she wasn't in trouble, after all.

"When I heard about what happened at the station today, well," said Jasper, shaking his head. "I don't think I've ever been so concerned for anyone as I was for you in that moment."

"If it's any consolation," said Felicity, "I, too, was rather concerned for my welfare at a certain point."

Jasper didn't find Felicity's attempt at humour remotely amusing. He sighed again. "There's a balance to be struck between wanting to take care of you and encouraging you to be your own independent person. I'm not sure I've always got that balance right, but I would like to keep trying. Therefore, I have a proposal."

Felicity arced an eyebrow. "What kind of proposal?"

"I have a vacancy for you. At the Western Daily News. You'll be a news reporter." He held up a hand to pre-empt any protest. "Not a trainee."

"I won't be shadowing anyone?" Felicity's mind jumped to Alex. Working with him hadn't been so bad.

"No. No shadowing."

Felicity sat taller in her chair. "And what will I be reporting on?"

"General news across Devon and the surrounding areas. Things like the opening of a new public park, or the results of the competitions at the annual county show. Perhaps a cliff rescue at the seaside. It'll be very different to your work as a society reporter, that's for certain. You'll travel much more, and you'll be writing to stricter deadlines. You'll be a news reporter like the rest of them, except in one respect."

"What's that?"

"You'll cover no crime stories. And certainly no violent crime."

Felicity paused, considering her brother's proposal. "Who'll be writing the crime stories?"

Jasper took up his pipe and relit it. "I'm going to be giving a lot more of them to Coop. He's done a splendid job keeping on top of the Reeves case. Some of the best circulation figures we've had in many months. It's also an area in which he seems quite interested in specialising."

"So he's staying on at the News?"

Jasper puffed on his pipe and nodded.

A little thrill passed through Felicity. Wasn't this exactly what she wanted?

"Why can't I cover crime stories?" she said. "I already have experience."

Jasper frowned. "A bit too much experience for my liking, Cici." He paused as he put his pipe back in the ashtray. "You have the Quick family trait all right, and perhaps one day you'll make a rather excellent crime reporter. But you might forgive your elder brother if that day isn't today."

Felicity thought for a moment. She was thankful for how loving her family was, and despite their disagreements, she knew she was lucky to have her brother looking out for her. However, that didn't leave her under any obligation to make things easy for him. "I'll accept your offer," she said, "on one condition."

Jasper leaned back in his chair, pulled on his pipe, and narrowed his eyes. "And what might that be?"

Chapter Thirty-Two

LOWER DIDDLETON'S VILLAGE GREEN, THREE WEEKS LATER

"Is that Ophelia? Something of an obvious choice. Don't you think so, dear?"

Felicity stood beside her grandmother on the village green. Before them was a row of roses, their long stems clipped and arranged in identical glass vases, ready for judgement in the flower competition at Lower Diddleton's summer fete.

Felicity leaned in and inhaled the roses' delicious perfume. She had on a light summer dress in white with tiny blue beads embellishing the neck and hem, and a white musketeer hat decorated with pale blue flowers. Tucked under her arm was Pip, his black button nose twitching towards the flowers.

"I find all roses beautiful," she said.

Lady Henrietta sighed and spoke in low tones as she continued to critique the competition."I suppose people will always have a soft spot for pink when it comes to roses." She was cooling herself with a large lace fan, refusing to give up on her long, high-necked dresses even in the hottest of weather. "But my Soleil d'Ors have so much more going for them. There are more blooms per stem, and the—" Lady Henrietta interrupted herself, her manner changing rather dramatically. "Oh, Mrs Winterpole. How delightful to see you," she said as the woman in question approached the show bench. "What an absolutely stunning display. Your Ophelias are a triumph. Lower Diddleton's Plant and Floral Society has outdone itself once again."

Mrs Winterpole nodded proudly. "Thank you, Lady Henrietta, but it's not just the roses that are a triumph, is it? Why, at times I imagined we wouldn't even have a fete this year. Isn't it wonderful to see the village restored to normality?"

"Oh, indeed, Mrs Winterpole," said Lady Henrietta, following her rival's gaze across the green. "Indeed."

The weather was splendidly sunny, with just a couple of fluffy white clouds in a rich blue sky. Horse and cart rides full of day-trippers were circling the village green. In the shade of one of the green's mighty oaks, Mr and Mrs Fry had a large table of baked goods for sale, including scones they were serving with clotted cream and jam, which were proving very popular with the tourists. Besides prizes for roses and fuchsias — with Lady Northcote dominating the competition in the latter category — there were also tables of marrows, onions, and other vegetables awaiting judgement. Lord Northcote had also brought several of his impeccably trained gun dogs to put on an obedience display, and onlookers offered gentle applause as the well-trained spaniels waited, fetched, and returned, toy ducks gently clasped in their mouths. The elderly Heather watched misty-eyed from the sidelines and offered the occasional whimper.

"We have quite some newcomers at this year's fete, wouldn't you say?" suggested Felicity.

"I've never known it so busy," confirmed Mrs Winterpole. "Perhaps it comes from Lower Diddleton being in the newspapers so much, although we'd rather none of that awful business ever happened."

Sergeant Hodgkins and Constable Price were patrolling the village green, their faces serious as they scanned the crowds. They nodded curtly towards Felicity, Lady Henrietta, and Mrs Winterpole.

"I mean, we've never had the police patrolling at the fete before," continued Mrs Winterpole, "but I suppose we must be grateful for their presence."

"I can't say I've ever enjoyed spending time in crowds," said Lady Henrietta, "but I can imagine the local businesses must be pleased with the extra influx." She nodded towards the cobbled yard of the Cat and Cream. It was bursting with people, with Mr Chesterton rushing from table to table, attending to clients and issuing orders to his serving staff.

"Will you be entering Master Pip in the dog show, Lady Felicity?" enquired Mrs Winterpole.

"Goodness, no," responded Felicity. She looked down at Pip, who was eyeing a passing poodle in an unfriendly manner. "He can be awfully poorly behaved when mixing with other canines, and he considers himself rather above competitive endeavours. Besides, I have work to do. The vicar's expecting a piece from me on the fete for the parish newsletter."

Felicity was indeed busier than ever, dividing her time between the newsletter and the Western Daily News, the vicar having persuaded her to continue contributing to the parish newsletter while he sought a new editor.

Mrs Winterpole nodded knowingly. "You do write so extremely well, Lady Felicity. I've read your pieces in the News as well. Especially that one about the victim and his murderer, and how the two came to be linked."

The condition Felicity had given her brother for accepting her new position on his newspaper was that she would be allowed to write one article about the Reeves case. After some thought, Jasper had accepted the condition, and Felicity had written a piece that delved into the personal backgrounds of Mr Reeves and his murderer.

"Oh?" said Felicity, setting a wriggling Pip on the ground so that he could chase after the scone crumbs being dropped from nearby paper plates. "What did you think?"

Mrs Winterpole tutted. "Who would have suspected that we had a blackmailer among us? And such a prolific one, at that. At it for years, wasn't he? And although I can't have sympathy for a murderer, to have grown up in poverty without a father, and then to have had your mother taken away at such a young age..." She shook her head. "Tragic."

"It's an exceedingly sad story," agreed Felicity. "In so many ways."

She'd written several articles for the News over the last couple of weeks, including one about a new bus route crossing the moors and a piece about plans for a potential motor racing circuit near Plymouth. But it was the background article she'd written on Mr Reeves and his murderer that seemed to have touched people most. It was also the article she'd most enjoyed writing, even though the story itself was extremely bleak.

"The newspaper's doing well, I must say," said Lady Henrietta. "Pity Jasper couldn't make it to the fete, but those meetings in London are going to be interesting."

"Oh?" said Mrs Winterpole. "What's happening in London?"

Felicity smiled, proud of her family's achievements. "Jasper's talking to the big national dailies about syndicating the articles we publish in the Western Daily News. They were rather impressed by our reporting in the wake of Mr Reeves' murder. They'd like to share our stories with a wider audience."

"Yes, that new journalist is doing a rather splendid job, wouldn't you say?" said Felicity's grandmother. "What's his name again? A friend of Jasper's from the war, wasn't he?"

"His name's Alexander Cooper," Felicity said, with only a small amount of hesitation. She hadn't seen him since the incident at Sweetbrooke station. She hadn't expected to, really, although she'd been disappointed on the occasions she'd visited the newspaper's offices in Exeter and found him absent. His articles were indeed extremely good. Felicity had read all of them, but it gave her an odd feeling to think about him, as if business between the two of them wasn't finished. If Felicity were ever to see Alex again, she was determined to make a point of thanking him properly for all he'd done for her.

"That's the one. Brilliant boy," said Lady Henrietta, who had the tendency to refer to any man under the age of sixty as a boy. "Jasper was, of course, also extremely clever to take him on. And to take you on as well, dear." Lady Henrietta put a reassuring hand on Felicity's arm. "The News is going from strength to strength with so many young, intelligent people on board."

Felicity smiled at her grandmother, who'd recently become much less opposed to the idea of her career as a journalist. Felicity rather suspected a few words from Jasper had influenced her in that regard.

"I'm terribly sorry to interrupt, Lady Felicity," said Mrs Winterpole, "but it looks as though your attention is needed elsewhere."

On the other side of the green, beyond the duck pond, stood the vicar, who was head and shoulders taller than many of his parishioners. He was waving and beckoning Felicity towards him, his wispy hair fluttering in the breeze. Felicity glanced at the church tower. It was nearly eleven o'clock.

"Of course," she said. "The egg-and-spoon race is about to start. I promised I'd be there to cover it for the parish newsletter. Would you watch Pip, please, Grandmama?" The little Yorkie was under a trestle table, gnawing on a dropped cherry slice. "Could you perhaps ensure he doesn't eat too many sweet treats?"

"I'll do my best, dear, but it can be difficult not to let Master Pip have his own way. Now go," said Lady Henrietta with a shooing motion, "before the starting gun goes off without you."

Already pulling her notepad from her pocket, Felicity hurried towards the other side of the village green. She dodged a group of people celebrating a win at the coconut shy, squeezed through the queue for a dart board covered in playing cards that seemed to offer some high prizes, and circumvented a helter skelter in bright red and yellow that was proving immensely popular with the younger children. It was all going well until a mistimed side-step had her collide into the back of a tall man in a light grey pinstriped suit. Felicity's notepad fell onto the grass.

"Heavens," she said, bending to collect her notepad. "I'm so terribly sorry."

"No need to be sorry. I was hoping I might see you today."

As Felicity straightened herself, she met the calm, blue gaze of Alex Cooper.

A flood of things she could say to him rushed through her mind. How deeply thankful she was for how he'd saved her that day at Sweetbrooke station, how grateful she was that Jasper still didn't know about her midnight visit to the churchyard, how truly excellent his articles were, how working with him hadn't been bad at all, it had actually been rather fun.

"Um," was the only sound she could manage, and it wasn't even a word.

"I'm Alex Cooper. I'm a news reporter for your brother's paper. We worked together for a short time on the Reeves story." His brow creased a little. "Remember?"

Felicity gave her head a shake, snapping herself out of her trance. "How dreadfully rude of me," she said, the power of speech now returned to her. "Of course I know who you are. How could I possibly ever forget?"

Alex smiled. "How are you doing these days, Felicity?"

She waved a hand towards the vicar to tell him she was on her way. "Busy," she said. "I've got an egg-and-spoon race to cover in, oh, approximately thirty seconds from now."

"Don't let me hold you up. I'm just glad you're doing well."

"No, no. You're not holding me up. I, um... What are you doing here? Are you covering the fete?"

"Day off. Took the train from Exeter. Wanted to see a bit more of the countryside."

"So you're enjoying it down here? You don't miss London too much?"

"Can't say that I do. Plenty of action in Devon. And you can't beat the scenery," he said with a glance at the cottages and tall trees that surrounded the village green, and the rolling fields beyond.

Felicity smiled. "Are you staying on for lunch?"

"That was the plan."

Again, Felicity waved towards the vicar, who was practically hopping up and down. "I really have to dash, but would you like to lunch together? We could get a table at the Cat and Cream. Or, failing that, a scone or two from the Frys."

Alex beamed. He had a rather winsome smile. "I'd like that very much."

The starting pistol for the egg-and-spoon race went off.

"Got to run!" said Felicity, waving at Alex as she dashed off through the crowds.

When she arrived on the sidelines of the race, her insides were all aflutter.

Claim your free Lady Felicity Quick ebook!

Sign up for my email newsletter and you'll get **Murder at Afternoon Tea** absolutely free.

This exclusive story isn't available anywhere else.

As a newsletter subscriber, you'll also receive writing updates, special offers, and peeks behind the scenes...

Use this link to sign up and claim your copy today:
https://BookHip.com/XMGPNZC

Read the next in the series...

Murder at a Country House

A Lady Felicity Quick 1920s Cozy Mystery
Book 2

Langton Manor is a traditional British country estate, with a grand ballroom, elegant gardens, a retinue of servants ... and a murder or two!

England, 1921. When journalist Lady Felicity Quick arrives at Langton Manor to discover her interview with pleasant-but-dull Lord Langton has been cancelled, Felicity is rather relieved — until she learns the reason is murder.

Trapped at the remote country house as thick fog descends, and surrounded by Lord Langton's bickering relatives, who seem more concerned with their own problems than the untimely death, Felicity develops her own theories about who might be responsible for the crime.

But when the life of someone she cares about is threatened, Felicity can sit by no longer. With the killer still at Langton Manor, and the police unable to reach them, can Felicity use her investigative skills to unmask the murderer and prevent further carnage?

If you love puzzling country house murders set in the old-fashioned elegance of 1920s England, then you will love this cozy mystery series! For fans of Agatha Christie, Downton Abbey, Lee Strauss, and Benedict Brown.

Read Murder at a Country House today!
getbook.at/countryhouse

The Lady Felicity Quick Mystery Series

Murder at Afternoon Tea

(Novella | Exclusive for Newsletter Subscribers)

Murder on the Village Green

(Book 1 | Available Now)

Murder at a Country House

(Book 2 | Available Now)

Murder at the Tea Rooms

(Book 3 | Available Now)

Murder at the Ball

(Book 4 | Available Now)

Murder on the Coast

(Book 5 | Available Now)

Murder at a Boarding School

(Book 6 | Coming Soon)

About the Author

Rosie Hunt is a British author of cozy mysteries both puzzling and historical. Her books include the Lady Felicity Quick mystery series set in the green and pleasant countryside of southwest England in the 1920s.

A history addict and former journalist, Rosie grew up immersed in the worlds of Poirot and Miss Marple. This early exposure to baffling murder mysteries rather coloured her outlook on life, and it was only a matter of time before she began writing her own.

Rosie loves clotted cream, knitting, and Golden Age crime fiction, and she'll never miss an opportunity to visit a National Trust property. She lives with her husband and their four-pawed overlord on a river in Northern Europe.

Join Rosie's mailing list:
bookhip.com/XMGPNZC

Follow Rosie on Facebook:
facebook.com/RosieHuntAuthor

Printed in Great Britain
by Amazon

39565895R00128